TMNT™

MOVIE NOVELIZATION

"A *sensei* once counseled a grief-stricken boy as his older brother prepared to leave for battle. He said, 'Child, why do you cry? You are both part of a *family*. And a family is a bond that cannot be broken by war, by strife, by force or neglect. And, more important, you are *brothers*. And brothers you shall remain, despite time . . . argument . . . and even distance.'"

—*Splinter the rat*

TMNT™

MOVIE NOVELIZATION

Adapted by Steve Murphy
Based on the screenplay by Kevin Munroe

Simon Spotlight
New York   London   Toronto   Sydney

Based on the film TMNT™ by Imagi Animation Studios and Warner Bros.

SIMON SPOTLIGHT
An imprint of Simon & Schuster Children's Publishing Division
1230 Avenue of the Americas, New York, New York 10020
© 2007 Mirage Studios, Inc. *Teenage Mutant Ninja Turtles*™ and *TMNT*™ are trademarks of Mirage Studios, Inc.
All rights reserved.

SIMON SPOTLIGHT and colophon are registered trademarks of Simon & Schuster, Inc. All rights reserved, including the right of reproduction in whole or in part in any form.
Manufactured in the United States of America
First Edition
1 2 3 4 5 6 7 8 9 10
ISBN-13: 978-1-4169-4057-9
ISBN-10: 1-4169-4057-X

PROLOGUE
LEONARDO'S JOURNEY

He was a stranger to these stars.

Out here in the rain forest, hundreds of miles from any significant human light source, the night sky is filled with more stars than I've ever imagined. This far south there are stars and constellations that I've never seen before. Like that group of stars there, low on the northern horizon. It looks like a curving snake. Weird. I've been looking at this sky for nearly a month now. . . . It almost seems as though the snake has been trying to straighten itself. Is that possible? I wish I knew more about astronomy, the way the universe is structured. . . .

Leonardo shut his eyes and began to inhale and exhale slowly and deeply. It was time for his final meditation of the day. Time to banish all thought, to ignore the physical reality that engulfed him—the sky, the tropical rain forest, the soft whisperings of passing bats, and his hammock, slung three hundred feet above the ground in the canopy of a silk-cotton tree.

Suddenly a thought long tucked away entered his consciousness: home. It's almost time to return home. Leonardo smiled before once again beginning the process of emptying his mind, of heading down his now nearly effortless path toward *Samadhi*—the universal consciousness of no mind.

Just then he heard gunshots ring out. They seemed to be coming from a village not far from where he was. And Leonardo knew his time for quiet and calm would have to wait.

"We appreciate your generous donations for the continued protection of your village," said a heavy-set man to a cowering group of villagers. "After all, the jungle can be a very dangerous place. Bah-ha-ha-ha-ha!"

The man's two assistants joined him in maniacal laughter as the villagers—men, women, and children—

gave them what few items of value they owned. The men's jeep was already overflowing with all their crops.

The heartless villains were *criministas*, members of a paramilitary group that preyed on villages outside the government's protection. They were each armed with a machine gun.

Pantera, the leader, pointed to a necklace worn by one of the women. "Your necklace. Bring it to me," he ordered.

"But this . . . this is a family heirloom," said the woman, standing her ground.

"Cortez, Brizuela," Pantera called to his henchmen. "Bring the necklace *and* the woman to me. *Now*."

The two began to approach the woman when suddenly—*whoosh*! All anyone saw was a glint of metal in the moonlight, then the arc of a heavy metal chain as it flew through the air and wrapped itself around the necks of both men. Cortez and Brizuela immediately dropped to the ground, unconscious.

Shocked, Pantera and the villagers looked toward the edge of the forest.

"The ghost of the jungle," whispered a young boy. His initial fear quickly gave way to feelings of hope. "The jungle god that punishes those who prey upon the weak."

"Show yourself!" shouted Pantera, still staring at the forest as he inched toward his jeep. "I am not afraid of a myth. I am not afraid of a ghost."

At that moment a pair of eyes opened in the darkness behind him. "Actually . . . I'm a Turtle, pal," said Leonardo with a grin, one hand wielding his katana.

Pantera swung around, raising his machine gun to shoot, but all it took was a swift kick and the gun sailed out of his hands.

"You . . . you are no ghost," stammered Pantera, reaching for a pistol hidden within his belt.

"And you," said Leonardo, kicking the pistol from Pantera's hand, "are no man."

Leonardo leaped straight into the air, simultaneously sheathing his katana and delivering a roundhouse kick to Pantera's jaw.

With a groan Pantera fell to the ground and passed out.

"The ghost of the jungle!" shouted the same boy, rushing toward Leonardo.

"Not a ghost," said Leonardo, before fading out of sight of the approaching villagers, "a ninja."

Whose training is now complete, the Turtle thought.

CHAPTER 1
ENTER THE NIGHTWATCHER

The mugger ran as fast as he could, putting increasing distance between himself and the three police officers who pursued him. He was young and fit, and soon safely beyond their grasp. Realizing that they were never going to nab him, the cops gave up the chase.

"Heh, heh . . . suckers," the mugger said to himself, as he slowed his pace. He intended to blend in with the people who were still out at this time of night in the Chelsea section of Manhattan. Good thing this city never sleeps, he thought.

He paused to glance back at the policemen—and did a double take. A jet-black racing motorcycle was flying in midair over the policemen's heads. Worse, it was heading directly toward him!

The mugger sprinted forward, but it was too late.

The motorcycle was moving too fast and caught up with him in seconds.

Gripping one end of a heavy chain, the motorcycle rider, fully dressed in black leather gear and a black-visored helmet, whipped the chain around the mugger's neck and arm, lifting him off the ground.

"You crazy? Put me down, man!" yelled the mugger.

But the rider didn't—not until after he plowed his victim's head into every trash can along Ninth Avenue. Then he left the mugger in front of a police station and headed east. He looked out for criminal activity and police chases as he looped his bike across the city, toward the Lower East Side.

Entering a deserted street, the motorcycle came to a screeching halt in front of a closed newsstand.

The motorcyclist, his face hidden by darkness, lifted his visor to scan the headlines of the newspapers that were still on display: "Woman Mysteriously Rescued From Burning Building," "Police Seek Motorcyclist Known As 'The Nightwatcher' for Questioning," "Who Is the Nightwatcher?"

Chuckling at the last headline, the rider removed his helmet and freed the two hanging ends of his red bandana.

"Love it," said Raphael. "'Nightwatcher' definitely has a nice ring to it."

Then, strapping his helmet back on, he revved the motorcycle's powerful V-twin engine, let out the clutch, and roared away.

If Leonardo could only see me now, Raphael thought, feeling very pleased with himself.

CHAPTER 2
THE TWO HEADS OF COWABUNGA CARL

Michelangelo's eyes were wide with fear. "Dude, they're all around me! What do I do? What do I do?" he whispered desperately.

"Just relax, Mikey. Remember your training. You'll be fine," Donatello's voice cooed into Michelangelo's headset.

Ten children wearing birthday hats rushed at Michelangelo, waving their foam nunchakus. Inside the oversize Turtle mascot head that he wore, Michelangelo let out a deep sigh as he braced for the onslaught.

"Get him!" screamed a small girl in pigtails. "Get Cowabunga Carl!"

"Take that, Turtle-dork," taunted a boy as he repeatedly slapped the nunchakus at Michelangelo's thighs. Two other boys tackled Michelangelo's legs.

Michelangelo fell to his knees. "Ow! That hurt!"

Then as suddenly as they appeared, the children disappeared, heading off to another part of the house, screaming "Cake!"

"Can I leave now?" Michelangelo whispered again, as he lay on the ground.

"Be cool," said Donatello. "Munchkin at two o'clock, closing fast."

The same pigtailed little girl ran up to Cowabunga Carl and kicked him, shouting "Kee-yah!" Hurrying toward the kitchen, she exclaimed, "This is the best birthday ever, Mommy!"

After a few minutes, Michelangelo slowly stood up, rubbing the pain out of his thighs. "There has got to be an easier way to make a living," he said.

A woman walked up to him. "Cowabunga Carl," she said. "You were terrific, absolutely terrific."

Then she pressed a cash-filled envelope into Michelangelo's hand, and the Turtle instantly felt better.

Leaving the apartment, Michelangelo walked out of the building and headed for a van parked in front. It had a huge cartoon Turtle face painted on its sides above the words COWABUNGA CARL.

Donatello opened the van's rear doors and helped

Michelangelo remove his Cowabunga Carl head. He then peeled off the fake zipper that was glued down the center of his brother's plastron. When Donatello was done, Michelangelo slumped onto the passenger seat, exhausted.

"Isn't this so much fun, Mikey?" Donatello asked, shutting the doors. "I mean, *Carl*," he added, laughing. "Plus, it pays pretty well."

"True dat," agreed Michelangelo.

Michelangelo reached into his belt and pulled out the envelope and another thick wad of bills. While Michelangelo counted the day's earnings, Donatello drove southward, finally pulling the van up to several abandoned warehouses. He pressed a remote control button, which opened a huge gate. Donatello drove the van into the warehouse and made sure the gate was shut before the two brothers exited the van.

Entering a trapdoor hidden on the warehouse floor, Michelangelo announced, "Honeeeeeey! I'm hooooome!" before kicking open the double doors to the Turtles' sewer lair.

"Moneymoneymoneymoney," chimed Donatello. "I'm going to buy a new framizat with my share of the loot. We'll have central air in here in no time."

"I still wish you'd invent a robot maid to do our

chores," Michelangelo replied, throwing himself onto a sofa and turning on the TV.

"Michelangelo!" a voice called out.

Michelangelo immediately shut off the TV and snapped to an obedient standing pose. "Yes, *Sensei*."

Splinter, their teacher and father to the four Turtles, entered the room. He pointed at Michelangelo with his walking stick. "Well?"

"*Sensei*?" asked the Turtle, puzzled, before blurting, "Oh!"

With a grin, Michelangelo reached into his duffle bag and pulled out a foil-wrapped piece of birthday cake. "Here you go, master."

"Ahh, butter-cream frosting!" noted Splinter happily as he uncovered the sweet treat. "My favorite."

CHAPTER 3
ALONE TOGETHER

The *San Felipe* had recently arrived from Belize and was now docked at a pier in Jersey City. A large crane lowered the last item from its cargo hold, a heavy eight-foot-tall crate with the words O'NEIL CARGO stenciled on its side panels.

The crate landed heavily.

"Careful! That isn't a box full of fish!" yelled April O'Neil as she approached the crate. That's the last one, she reminded herself proudly.

April pulled out her cell phone and hit a speed dial number. On the other end, a phone rang . . . and rang and rang.

"Where are you, Casey?" April said impatiently.

In the Red Hook neighborhood of Brooklyn, Casey Jones lay asleep on the couch of the apartment he shared with April. His snoring was loud enough to be heard over the sound of his TV set, which was turned to near-peak volume. The ringing telephone didn't stand a chance. Not until several seconds of dead air filled the space between commercials.

Ring.

"Wha—?" mumbled Casey, groggily.

Ring.

"The telephone? Aw, man, where'd I leave the telephone?" he said, slowly pulling himself off the couch.

Ring.

Casey staggered across the spacious loft apartment. Overflowing bookcases divided the space into several rooms. Unopened crates topped with open maps and dog-eared guidebooks filled one area, while another contained a set of free weights, a rowing machine, and messy stacks of magazines.

Ring.

"Ah, the kitchen," Casey said as he made his way toward the sound of the ringing phone, side-stepping the piles of soiled clothing that lay strewn across the floor.

Ring.

Casey entered the kitchen, where a stack of empty pizza boxes looked like a model for the

Leaning Tower of Pisa. Dirty dishes covered every inch of counter space.

Ring.

"Ah, there you are," said Casey, reaching into the sink.

"Talk to me," he said into the phone.

"Hey, it's me," April said. "I'm back."

Casey slapped himself on the forehead. April! And she sounds ticked-off.

"Uh, was that today, babe?" he asked, scratching his armpit.

April paused for a second before responding.

"Yes, it was today that I returned to you after being in a deadly jungle for nearly a month," replied April, disappointed. "I thought you were going to meet me dockside?"

"I'm sorry, babe. I must've—"

April didn't want to hear any more. "Forget it. I'll take a cab," she said icily before hanging up.

Casey put the phone back in the sink. "Good goin', Case," he muttered, angrily kicking over the teetering tower of pizza boxes.

CHAPTER 4
FAMILY REUNION

"**I**'m bored!" Michelangelo complained dramatically as he entered Donatello's room.

Donatello ignored him as he sat hunched over a worktable. Past inventions in various stages of completion lined the walls of his room. Piles of hardware shared floor space with wires and power cords, which were curled and twisted throughout the room like giant strands of spaghetti.

"Don, you ever feel like you were meant for more? I mean, sometimes I feel like we never even left that glass turtle bowl when we were little dudes. I mean, every day it's the same thing."

Donatello turned to face his brother. His eyes were magnified through his work goggles, giving him the appearance of an insect. "Oh, hi, Mikey," said Donatello. "You say something?"

Michelangelo stared at Donatello and tried his best not to say anything mean before turning and walking out of the room. He did a backflip onto the living room couch and shut his eyes, only to open them a moment later, surprised to find Splinter seated next to him. The Turtle had not heard his master approach, and here he was, sitting cross-legged and calmly sipping a cup of tea.

"Michelangelo," said Splinter. "Boredom is never an indicator of your surroundings. It is only a reflection of your inner heart. Fill yourself with excitement on the inside, and you'll live the most rewarding life of all."

Michelangelo adopted a thoughtful expression and again kept himself from saying something he'd later regret. "Yes, master," he replied humbly.

After Splinter left the room, Michelangelo turned on the TV. A news reporter was in the middle of a report:

"And so yet again, police officials are baffled at a crime of retribution that can only be attributed to the mysterious figure known as the Nightwatcher. This is the latest in a string of vigilante acts that have been plaguing the city for the past year. Although the victims have been criminals, the Nightwatcher's actions have been described as overly violent, verging on the edge of lethal."

Michelangelo reached for the Polaroid camera on the table in front of the couch and took a picture of the reporter. He turned off the TV and waited for the photo to develop.

When the reporter's face appeared on the photo, Michelangelo reached under the couch and pulled out a scrapbook. It was overflowing with newspaper clippings on the city's latest vigilante. Michelangelo placed the picture on a blank page.

"Now *that's* what I'm talking about! Cruising the streets, busting the noggins of those who hold themselves above the law." Then, impersonating an announcer's voice, Michelangelo added, "but they aren't above *his* law."

Donatello walked into the living room with an invention in one hand. "But Mikey, the man's a criminal himself. Anyone who operates without boundary or rule of law cannot be legislated and therefore must be reined in."

"Sounds like four Turtles I used to know," said Raphael, joining his brothers. He stared at Donatello. "What's your beef with puttin' dirtbags behind bars, Donnie?"

"I have no problem with the incarceration of those who deserve it, but who makes sure that the Nightwatcher doesn't cross the line?" Donatello asked.

"Well, I think he's the shot in the arm this city needs," said Raphael. "The way *we* should be."

With his chest thrust out, Raphael swaggered over to Donatello. "Sometimes there are lines that even the police can't cross," he added. "Someone has to be willing to do so. And to do that, *fear* becomes a weapon."

"You are such a Neanderthal," replied Donatello, taking a step back.

Raphael faked a lunge at Donatello, who was startled by his brother's unexpected move.

"I rest my case," Raphael said, grinning.

"Raphael!" scolded Splinter. "If bullying is the only way to argue your point, then perhaps you do not have much of a point to begin with. And where have you been? You've been spending so much time away from home lately. . . ."

Raphael looked down. "Sorry, master."

Then, without saying another word, Raphael left the living room. He did not join his two brothers and *sensei* for supper or for the evening's meditation.

That night Splinter kept the door to his room open. Every so often he would peer out into the darkened hallway, then return to kneel on the floor of his dimly lit room.

A figure soon appeared at the doorway.

"Enter," said the rat.

Leonardo strode into the room and kneeled facing his *sensei*, head lowered in a respectful bow. "I have returned from the rain forest, master. I have completed my year's training. I am prepared for the next stage."

Splinter looked fondly at Leonardo. "That you are, my son," he said with pride. "You must now apply all that you have learned on your lengthy journey to your everyday life. *That* will be the most challenging training of all."

He handed an ancient medallion to Leonardo. "You have done very well, my son. You have earned this ten times over."

Hearing Leonardo's voice, Raphael had stepped out of his room and was now watching the scene with jealousy.

"I've missed you, Leonardo," said Splinter, getting to his feet.

Leonardo stood up. "I've missed you too, father."

The two embraced.

"I'm afraid that much has changed in your brothers' spirits since you left home," Splinter said. "But now that you have returned, they will have the ethical and warrior leadership they have been lacking. The family needs you. Do you understand?"

"I . . . I do, *Sensei*," replied Leonardo, swallowing hard.

Even though Splinter could not see Raphael, he sensed his presence. "Raphael," he said toward the doorway. "Your brother is home."

Raphael stepped into the room, trying hard not to look embarrassed at being caught.

Leonardo and Raphael faced each other awkwardly.

"Hey," said Leonardo.

"Hey," said Raphael, eyes firmly affixed on his brother's medallion. "Congratulations."

"Thanks," said Leonardo.

Raphael looked at his brother and father. "Well, I'm heading back to bed," he said, feigning a yawn before slipping back down the hallway.

CHAPTER 5
TOWER OF POWER

Winters awoke with a sudden jolt. His heart was racing and a sheen of cold perspiration covered his body. Images of claws and teeth, horns and tusks, blades and blood and clashing armies were vivid in his mind.

When he got his bearings, Winters breathed a sigh of relief. "A nightmare," he said. "Just another nightmare."

He rose from his oversize Poltrona Frau bed, which was designed exclusively for him. Winters looked around his bedroom and smiled. The room was a testament to the best in both modern and retro design: sleek chairs by Rehti, a couch by Swan, sixties lamps by Vico Magistretti, surrounded by walls of techno-tribal mosaics by Mos of Italy. His smoked-glass and stressed-steel skyscraper, Winters Tower, by the architect Rem Koolhaas, conveyed money, mystery, and power. Much like myself, Winters thought.

After his morning workout—a mixture of martial arts and American-style boxing—Winters showered and dressed. He exited the personal living space that filled most of the top floor of the tower and entered his office, a large austere space full of history books and warrior-themed artifacts and curios. Large bay windows over-looked the city in a sweeping view. He felt powerful.

Winters surveyed the city, then turned from the windows and pressed a button on the wall. The view outside the window began to change . . . to lower. The entire office began to slide down the exterior of the monolithic tower. The office was an elevator.

Power.

"Hey, what happened to the power?" Michelangelo asked as the lights and machines they were using suddenly went out.

"Nobody panic! I have it all under control!" replied Donatello, who was still in his lab.

"I smell smoke and a tinge of burning electrical wires," noted Leonardo.

"Under control! Under control!" yelled Donatello, before there was a sudden *boom*! The lights flickered back on for a few minutes.

Leonardo and Michelangelo watched Donatello scurry past them, his face and hands covered in black soot. "Heh," Donatello said sheepishly, "just working on installing the central air-conditioning. Nothing to worry about." He ducked into a crawl space.

Reasonably assured that Donatello did have everything under control, Leonardo asked Michelangelo, "So, what's up with April and Casey? I expected them to drop by after I got back."

Michelangelo shrugged his shoulders. "We don't see much of them anymore. April seems to be working a lot . . . and Casey seems to be, I don't know, *different* lately. Maybe he doesn't like having to put the toilet seat down now that they've moved in together."

"Casey at least still doing his hockey-mask thing?"

"Don't know, bro. Haven't noticed since the Nightwatcher entered the scene."

Leonardo cocked his head. "Nightwatcher? That some new comic book you're hooked on, Mikey?"

"This should explain most of it," said Raphael,

entering the room. He reached under the couch and pulled out Michelangelo's Nightwatcher scrapbook.

"The legacy of the city's newest superhero," he added, tossing the scrapbook to Leonardo. "Compliments of fanboy Mikey."

"Joke all you want, Raph," countered Michelangelo. "But train hard and eat your veggies, and one day you too can be as cool as the Nightwatcher, dude."

"I can only hope, Mikey. I can only hope . . . ," Raphael replied with a grin. He clearly enjoyed keeping his identity a secret, especially from his brothers.

Leonardo flipped through the scrapbook, his face registering disapproval. "This guy could bring heat on all of us if he keeps this up," he said grimly. "Showboating isn't a replacement for justice. It's just self-indulgence. Someone needs to talk to this thug."

Raphael stopped grinning. He was about to respond to Leonardo, but he headed to his room instead, shaking his head. He just doesn't get it, thought Raphael. None of them do. I bet Casey would understand. He was once all about being a vigilante.

Raphael entered his room and shut the door. He took a long look at the framed photo of himself and Casey Jones and wondered what his old friend was up to.

At that moment Casey Jones was in a defensive crouch. He and five teenage boys were in the middle of a street-hockey game, played in an alley. Trash cans acted as goal posts, and milk crates marked out the four corners of the rink.

"Hey, you're offsides!" Casey yelled.

"No way, Space-Case!" replied a boy who ran past him, maneuvering the tip of his hockey stick toward a tennis ball. Flicking his wrist, the boy shot the ball forward and into a trash can that was turned on its side.

"Score!" he yelled triumphantly. He held his hockey stick high above his head.

"Ah, whatever," replied Casey. "The game ain't over yet."

Just then a voice called out from the second-floor window of the apartment building across the street. "Bobby! It's time for dinner!"

"But Ma, we was just winning!" replied Bobby.

"Robert!" his mother shot back.

"Sorry, dudes," said Bobby, turning to leave.

"Busted!" said Casey, grinning. "Have fun with your mommy."

But Casey's cheerfulness was short-lived. Across the street, dressed in a dark business suit, stood April—holding up a white shirt and a tie.

"Aw, c'mon, April!" Casey pleaded. "We just started."

"Please, Miss O'Neil?" one of the boys chimed in. "Can't Casey stay and play for just five more minutes? Pleeeeease?"

"Not today, guys," said April. "Mr. Jones has to pretend to be an adult for a few hours."

Without another word, Casey ambled over to April and took his shirt and tie from her. They walked down the street together in silence.

After a while April said, "I need your help with a delivery."

Casey's mood lightened. April needed his help! Responding with his best impersonation of Arnold Schwarzenegger, he said, "Ah, so you need my *funtah-stick* muscles?"

But April wasn't amused. "Put your shirt and tie on," she responded, not even bothering to look at her boyfriend.

April is so uptight, Casey thought, *ever since returning from, um, wherever.* He pulled the shirt over his head and quickly put on his tie. Then he placed an arm over April's shoulder, hoping that the gesture would be returned with some show of warmth. But April continued to walk stiffly, so Casey removed his arm, feeling extremely unsure of what he could do to make things better between them.

They continued to walk in silence, all the way from the truck rental center, past the city docks, to the gleaming new Winters Tower.

"Mr. Winters, April O'Neil and her assistant are here," announced the receptionist into her headset when they arrived at the expansive lobby of Winters Tower. Every surface of the room, from the floor to the thirty-foot-high arched ceiling, was of copper-hued marble. The entire lobby floor was designed in the shape of a large Aztec calendar.

Casey stood several feet behind April, dressed in white shirt and tie. Behind him was the large crate that had been unloaded from the *San Felipe*.

"*Assistant?*" muttered Casey, pulling nervously at his tie. He looked around the vast space, filled with ancient weapons displayed in glass cases and fragile-looking vases on marble pedestals.

Winters's voice came over the intercom. "Send them in," he said.

April strode toward the open doors of Winters's

office. Casey struggled with the heavy crate, hurrying to match her pace.

"Miss O'Neil," greeted Winters. "You are a vision. Thirty days in the rain forest and beautiful as ever." He kissed her on both cheeks, and Casey could feel the blood rushing to his own.

"Hello, Max," said April. "This is my, uh, friend . . . Casey Jones."

"Hey, Chris, how's it going?" said Winters.

"Actually, it's Ca—," Casey started to say.

But Winters cut him off. "So how was your trip, April?" he asked.

"You know, typical," April replied breezily. "Corrupt government officials, double-crossing guides. All ending in a heart-pounding chase."

April and Winters laughed. Casey played with his shirt collar, feeling very uncomfortable.

"But it was all worth it, Max," April said, pausing for a moment before declaring, "I found it. The fourth General."

Winters smiled as April turned to Casey. "The crowbar please, Casey."

April twirled the crowbar in one hand, then with a single swift gesture cracked open the front panel of the crate. The panel fell to the floor with a muffled *thud*.

Winters approached the open crate, and April and Casey stepped back.

"The gods be praised," Winters whispered. He stared at what was inside: a seven-foot-tall figure of granite and obsidian, a warrior sheathed in armor styled after an eagle. Winters passed his hand over the figure's helmet.

"Max, can I ask you a question?" April ventured.

"Yes, of course," answered Winters, his gaze remaining on the stone warrior.

"I've been so grateful for the opportunities you've given me," she said. "I'd probably still be selling antique curios if not for you. But I have to ask. . . . Why the fascination with these particular works of art? I'd never even *heard* of the Legend of Yaotl until we met."

Winters moved away from the statue. He looked past April and Casey toward a suit of armor displayed on the office wall behind them.

"Well," he said, "let me tell you a story. . . ."

CHAPTER 6
THE LEGEND OF YAOTL

"It was a long time ago, April," began Winters, not bothering to address Casey. "Sometime during what Westerners have come to define as the year one thousand and six, B.C.E. Nearly three thousand years ago.

"It was a time long before the Mayans, the Aztecs, and even the Olmecs. It was a time of legends. A time of *greatness*. Into this world came the man named Yaotl, more a force of nature than a man. Yaotl the Mysterious. Yaotl the Conqueror. Yaotl and his four Warrior-Priest Generals.

"Starting in what is now central Brazil and moving northward, Yaotl and his four Generals pillaged every culture in their path. And for every culture they destroyed, they drank in all the magic and knowledge that culture had attained.

"They were like a hurricane, gathering more power and knowledge with each conquest."

April was spellbound by the story, and Winters himself seemed completely immersed in his tale.

"After decimating the Paxmec culture—the peaceful federation of city-states that predated the Olmecs—Yaotl and his four Generals set their sights on the remote and hidden city of Xalica. Xalica had a culture rich in arcane science, wondrous magic, and its own technology. Xalica, the sister culture to fabled Atlantis.

"It was like blood in the water for a predator like Yaotl. His army numbered nearly a million warriors strong. As they approached Xalica, Yaotl and his Generals used the knowledge they'd gained in black magic and sorcery to create the Shadow Gate.

"Timing their attack with the alignment of the Stars of Kikin, they used the Shadow Gate to open a portal from another world. A dark world called Cthula.

"An army of Cthulan monsters passed through the Shadow Gate: basilisks, chimera, sylphs, minotaurs, manticores, hydras, griffins, and more . . . and all of them were unleashed on Xalica. At least that was Yaotl's plan: to control the monsters and direct them against Xalica.

"But the monsters knew no side. They destroyed

the enemy . . . as well as Yaotl's own army. It was a bloodbath not to be seen upon this world again until the twentieth century.

"In the end, there were no victors. Just a handful of survivors. Yaotl destroyed the Shadow Gate before more monsters could cross over. But it was too late, much too late.

"Yaotl and his Generals were responsible for the eradication of the greatest culture the world has ever known and probably will ever know. The knowledge that was lost with the destruction of Xalica will never be found again . . . *never*," Winters said, finishing his tale in a whisper.

"Quite the story, Max," said April, poking Casey, who had fallen asleep. As Casey slowly opened his eyes and wiped the drool off his chin, April asked, "You don't think that this could be—"

Winters cut her off. "Oh, no, Miss O'Neil, not at all. Like you said, it's just a story."

Then returning his attention to the statue, Winters simply said, "The receptionist will pay your fee on the way out."

"Thanks, um, good-bye, Max," April said, grabbing Casey and making a quick exit from Winters' office.

Out in the lobby April stopped walking and turned

to face Casey. They stood near a podium holding an ancient Peruvian vase.

"Oh, no," said Casey, "it's *the look*. What did I do now?"

April wasted no time. "Casey Jones, I give you an opportunity. I give you the chance to become a better man. And what do you do with it? *You fall asleep!*"

"But it was a boring story!" exclaimed Casey, ready to unleash his pent-up anger. "And you know, like, if you were home for more than four days at a time, you'd see that I don't want any of this!"

April eyed the vase. "Casey, you'd better be careful—," she began to say, but Casey was on a roll.

"Here I am nice enough to help you out, dressed in this monkey getup. That *chica* out there called me your *assistant*, you called me your *friend*. I don't need this kind of grief!" he firmly declared, spreading his arms out. His right hand struck the vase, and it fell to the floor, immediately shattering into pieces.

In that instant security sirens blared to life and shutters came slamming down on all of the tower's windows and external doorways.

"Oops," said Casey, no longer filled with fury.

April rubbed her temples. "Give me strength," she muttered, "give me strength."

CHAPTER 7
OF NINJAS AND MONSTERS

"You can come out now," Winters said, after he had been studying the statue for several hours.

Four figures emerged silently from the shadows in one corner of his office. They were a woman wearing a cloak and a Japanese Noh mask, followed by three ninjas of the Foot Clan.

"Your talents are commendable, Karai," noted Winters, turning from the statue to face his visitors.

"As are yours," said the woman, removing her mask. "Most don't notice us until *we* decide they will."

"Well, I guess I'm just special that way," Winters said, smirking. "So, down to business. Aside from the other reasons for your visit to America, are you interested in the offer we discussed?"

The new leader of the Foot Clan lowered her gaze. "I must confess . . . I still don't know exactly what we are to do for you," she said.

Winters walked over to the window. In the city spread out below him, thousands of lights sparkled.

"I need the finely tuned eyes and stealth of your Foot Ninjas to monitor the city for me over the next few days," answered Winters. "Just keep your eyes peeled for anything strange."

Karai stood in silence for a moment, then looked over at Winters.

"What kind of *strange*?" she asked with an obvious tone of suspicion.

Winters looked at Karai, a smile his only answer.

Several blocks southeast of Winters Towers, a man stood near one of the base columns of the Brooklyn Bridge. He looked at his watch and frowned. A quarter to twelve, he thought. Where is he? Where is my ride? My shift starts in fifteen minutes. I can't be late for work again.

The area was dark and, except for himself, deserted. Aside from the hiss of vehicles passing overhead on the bridge, it was quiet—except for that strange mewing sound.

The man looked around to see who was making the sound. It was probably coming from the other side of the bridge column. Then just when there seemed to be complete silence, a cat leaped out of the shadows.

"Waaaahhh!" yelled the man, before spotting the small creature.

"Nearly scared me half to death, kitty," he said to the cat, stooping to stroke its fur. The cat purred.

Soon a car pulled up. Finally, thought the man, as he opened the door and got in. The cat was still purring as it watched the car drive off. But an instant later, it froze. Sensing danger, it turned to leap away—but it was too late. A thick, clawed arm shot out and grabbed the cat.

The cat's screech was cut off abruptly, followed by a few seconds of silence. And then something burped.

CHAPTER 8

CLOSE ENCOUNTER

"**D**oesn't *anybody* train anymore?" Leonardo asked loudly, lifting his head from the weight bench and looking around. He was alone in the work-out area of the lair.

"Just a sec, dude! I'm almost at level eighteen!" called Michelangelo, as he frantically pushed buttons on his video-game controller. Suddenly the sound of an explosion boomed from the TV. "Scratch that," said Michelangelo with a sigh. "Seventeen. Again."

Leonardo stood and called out. "Donnie!"

"In, uh, a few minutes, Leo," answered Donatello from his lab. "I'm in the middle of an—"

The sound of another explosion rang out, this time from the lab.

"Um . . . make that another hour," corrected Donatello.

Leonardo sighed, just as Splinter appeared at his side. "A true leader knows how to motivate his troops regardless of their *own* motivations," said the rat.

Leonardo thought for a moment, then walked over to the circuit-breaker box. Pulling down the lever, he instantly cut off all the power in the lair.

"Hey! What's going on?" Raphael called out.

"Who turned out the power?" asked Donatello. "My experiment!"

"Aw, my game!" yelled Michelangelo.

"No more games," Leonardo said sternly. "Everyone, topside! Now!"

Moments later four Turtles stood on a rooftop and looked out across the darkened city.

"I don't know, Leo. What do you want me to say?" asked Michelangelo. "Ever since the Nightwatcher came to town, we started keeping a lower profile up here, not to mention that the current TV season is pretty primo right now."

Leonardo patted Michelangelo's belly. "That's no excuse to let your training slip, Mikey. The Nightwatcher may think he can push the world around, but I can assure you that he won't influence the way *we* live any longer."

"Well, maybe someone like the Nightwatcher isn't lucky enough to take a yearlong vacation," said Raphael. "Crime doesn't take a holiday, Leo."

The two glared at each other.

Donatello stepped between them. "Okay, guys, calm down. Leo brought us up here so he could teach us some things he learned in the rain forest. So if we could all just—"

"I got a better idea," Michelangelo interrupted. "Let's play ninja tag. Two teams."

He pointed to a distant billboard. "The first team to touch old faithful over there—"

"Does the other team's chores for a week," finished Donatello.

"Deal," Leonardo and Raphael said at the same time.

"I'm with Leo!" blurted Michelangelo.

Donatello looked at his brothers. "Actually, I think you and I should team up," he told Michelangelo.

"You kiddin' me?" asked Michelangelo, scoffing. "I mean, no offense, bro, but you ain't exactly the biggest hitter on the bench."

Aware of the tension between Leonardo and Raphael, Donatello firmly said, "Trust me on this one, Mikey."

"A straight path puts the billboard at eight rooftops. Everyone ready?" asked Leonardo.

"I was born ready," answered Michelangelo.

"Then on your mark . . . get set . . . *go!*" shouted Leonardo.

The brothers ran and leaped off the rooftop, effortlessly sailing across the twenty feet that stretched between buildings. At first the teams were neck and neck. But by the fifth rooftop Raphael and Leonardo were half a rooftop ahead of Michelangelo and Donatello.

The sixth rooftop posed a bit of a challenge as it sloped east at a thirty-degree angle and was covered with a network of pipes and air ducts. Flat-out running wouldn't work here. Teamwork would.

Leonardo and Raphael slammed onto this rooftop and began sliding down its slope.

"Quick! Grab my hand!" Leonardo called out.

"No. You grab mine," replied Raphael.

Leonardo expected his brother to grab his hand, and when he didn't, Leonardo was forced to duck and roll—right into Raphael.

Raphael crashed face-first into a duct. Leonardo bounded over the duct and onto a pipe.

"You did that on purpose!" Raphael said accusingly.

"It was an accident," said Leonardo. "Wouldn't have happened if you grabbed my hand."

Raphael climbed on top of the duct and looked over at the next rooftop. He had a plan. "The only way we're going to get over there is if I cannonball you over and then allow the momentum of my throw to bounce off that flagpole and up onto the rooftop behind you."

Leonardo considered this. "Sounds good except—"

Before Leonardo could finish his thought, Raphael grabbed his arm, then spun him around before launching him into the air.

"Whoaaaaaaa!" Leonardo shouted, as his shell skidded over the lip of the next rooftop, barely clearing it.

"You did that on purpose," said Leonardo, as he watched his brother bounce up off the flagpole and land at his side. They began to jog toward the last rooftop.

Raphael grinned. "No, I didn't," he said.

Leonardo looked intently at his brother. "What's up with you, Raph? Have you been avoiding me? I've barely seen you since I got home."

"I've been busy."

"I see," said Leonardo. "You're definitely not up-set at me or anything, right?"

"Why do you think that?"

"Because when your brother gets to go on a worldwide training mission, and you have to stay home . . . might upset me, too."

Raphael glowered. "You trying to make me mad?"

"I'm just saying, I'd understand if you were upset."

"You wouldn't understand the first thing about me, daddy's boy—ooof!"

Raphael had tripped over an old antenna mount, directly into Leonardo's path. Tumbling and rolling, the two began pushing at each other.

"Is *that* what this is about? You think Splinter likes me best?" asked Leonardo.

"You'd love that, wouldn't you?" Raphael shot back. Finally they stopped rolling and stood up, facing the billboard that had been their goal.

"Ahem. So nice of you to join us, gentledudes," said Michelangelo. He was sitting with Donatello on top of the billboard.

"And by the way," said Donatello, "I prefer the classic military corner tuck for my bedsheets."

They gave each other high fives before jumping

down to their brothers. Suddenly Michelangelo yelled out, "Yowzah! You dudes see that up there?"

He pointed at a building that was under construction several blocks away. Large shadows could be seen shuffling across the framed I beams of an open-air upper floor.

"So what now, captain?" Michelangelo asked Leonardo.

"We need a plan," Leonardo answered.

But Raphael did not want to wait for Leonardo to come up with a plan. He wanted immediate action.

"Later!" he called, gracefully backflipping off the rooftop.

"Raph!" Leonardo shouted, as he watched his brother disappear.

"Welcome home," Michelangelo and Donatello said.

Not wanting to leave Raphael to fend for himself, the other three Turtles followed their brother to the construction site. The four of them climbed up the scaffolding and waited just one floor below the one where they had seen the strange shadows.

Donatello peered into the floor and was suddenly struck with fear. He had just noticed claw marks etched deeply into the steel beams.

"I've got a bad feeling about this," he whispered.

The unfinished building was several dozen stories high. Most of its floors were half finished, some less. Huge open spaces lay between floors, holes that would later be filled with stairwells and elevator shafts.

Standing on one side of the building, the Turtles listened quietly for several minutes before Leonardo signaled for the group to proceed upward. When they reached the top floor, Michelangelo looked down.

"Well, the good news is that there are a bunch of Foot Ninja getting the snot kicked out of them. The bad news is what's kicking the snot out of them. . . . "

The other Turtles looked in on the floor below. What they saw was an incredible sight: Six Foot Ninja and their leader, Karai, were in the midst of a battle against a tall, hairy Bigfootlike monster—and the monster was easily brushing off the ninjitsu blows.

"An interesting conundrum," said Donatello. "Do we hold dear the value of life and help the Foot regardless of our tumultuous past?"

"I say we sit back and enjoy the show," said Michelangelo, turning to Leonardo. "What do you say, leader boy?"

Leonardo took a deep breath, taking the time to work out a battle plan.

"I say we kick butt," Raphael said decisively as he lunged forward to join in the fight. Leonardo rolled his eyes, annoyed that once again there was no other option but to follow Raphael's impulsive decision.

The sudden appearance of the four Turtles brought the battle to a stop—for a while. Then, quickly jolted from the confusion, Karai lunged at Leonardo with her katanas, setting off a series of stunning swordplay.

"Who are you?" asked Leonardo, impressed by Karai's abilities.

Karai did not answer. Instead she gestured to the Foot Ninja, then, feigning a sword swipe at Leonardo's legs, leaped over him. Within seconds Karai and her men disappeared, leaving the Turtles to face the monster by themselves.

The gargantuan creature lunged at them.

"Uh-oh," said Michelangelo. "We need a plan . . . and fast!"

"We can take him!" Raphael yelled as he threw himself at the creature. It grabbed Raphael by the ankle and threw him to the floor below.

"Or maybe not," Raphael conceded.

Then the monster lashed out at Leonardo, coming within inches of his throat. Leonardo retaliated with a kick at the monster's stomach, but that didn't do anything. The monster punched Leonardo hard on his plastron, the force of the blow sending the Turtle dangerously close to the edge of the building.

"I've got a plan," Leonardo told his brothers. "Let's bring the fight down to ground level. It may help even the odds a little."

"How are we going to do that?" asked Donatello.

"By getting this big guy angry enough to come after us," said Leonardo. He threw a two-by-four at the creature. Bull's-eye! The wooden plank struck the monster on the head. With a howl, it ran toward the Turtle, and Leonardo immediately jumped down to the floor below. The chase was on!

The Turtles took turns attacking the monster, leading it downward. Finally they reached ground level.

"What do we do now, Leo?" asked Michelangelo. Standing less than fifty feet away, the monster glowered at them before lumbering forward.

Leonardo was about to speak when a strange noise made him look up.

"Incoming!" he shouted. "Scatter!"

Kaboom! A pallet full of bricks and cement blocks came crashing to the ground—and the Turtles barely escaped! They quickly retreated into the shadows as smoke and dust filled the air. Blinding floodlights suddenly came on, and the creature stared dumbly at them.

Just then heavy footsteps could be heard heading toward the monster. Amidst the rubble, smoke, and bright lights, the Turtles couldn't see the four large humanlike shapes that emerged very clearly. Each of them appeared to have a red glow coming from within their inner core.

"What are they?" whispered Raphael.

If the Turtles could make out what had appeared, they would have been startled to see four living, breathing statues, each suited up in high-tech gear and wearing outfits with an animal theme: an ape, an eagle, a jaguar, and a serpent.

They heard the monster roar as it tried to battle its new opponents, but the struggle quickly ended, and then there was silence followed by the slam of huge steel doors. The sound of an engine revving up filled the air before receding into the night—and was replaced with police sirens.

The Turtles looked at each other and knew what their next step would be.

"Best save this for another day," said Leonardo, as he and his brothers disappeared into the sewers.

CHAPTER 9
THE STONE GENERALS

Max Winters walked down the darkened stairwell of his office building. Entering a cavernous and dimly lit secret basement below the lobby, he was greeted by Karai and her six ninjas.

"What seems to be the problem?" he asked.

Karai tried to remain calm. "The *problem* is that we were hired merely to patrol the city and report anything *strange* to you. You never said *anything* about monsters."

Winters grinned and reached into the shoulder bag he was carrying. The Foot tensed, ready to strike if provoked. Karai herself had placed a hand on the hilt of her short blade.

Winters took out a large brick of money and met Karai's gaze. "Consider your job duties redefined," he said. "Congratulations on your promotion."

He tossed the money brick toward Karai. *Shink!* She sliced the brick in midair and it fell to the floor, landing in two even piles. "We may be hired help to you, but you should never forget we are the Foot Clan," the Foot leader said coldly.

"Ooooh," said Winters, smirking. "How cute . . . and silly."

The Foot were not going to let this remark go unanswered. Each ninja withdrew a katana and rushed forward. But Karai somersaulted ahead of her soldiers with her sword drawn. She placed its steel edge at Winters' throat.

Winters, however, remained unnerved. Instead he laughed.

At that moment four pairs of footsteps lumbered forward, revealing themselves as they stood behind Winters. They were the same animal-humanoid figures from the construction site.

"May I introduce the four Stone Generals," Winters said calmly to Karai, even as her blade was still pressed at his throat. "Mono the ape, Aguila the eagle, Gato the jaguar, and Serpiente . . . well, it's obvious what she is."

The Generals smiled and glowed red. Mono lifted a huge hammer in salute.

"We made a deal, Karai. I expect you to honor it," said Winters. "You do understand 'honor,' don't you?"

He stared at her for a moment before adding, "I don't care what part of 'muscle for hire' you don't understand. I hired your muscle. Now exercise the ones attached to your feet and get back to work."

Karai stepped back slowly, and Winters widened his smile.

"I will triple your pay for your troubles. Are we cool now?" he asked, withdrawing several stacks of bills from his bag.

Karai nodded tersely.

"Ninjas. No sense of humor," Winters muttered before turning to face the Generals.

"Were there any problems?" he asked, addressing Aguila.

"None, my lord," answered Aguila, his voice deep and gravelly.

Karai looked at the four stone creatures. They reminded her of supernatural beings from a folktale she had heard in her childhood—a story almost as strange as the one that seemed to be unfolding before her. "Just what is this all about?" she asked.

"Oh, let's just call it a scavenger hunt. I now have the power and know-how," he said, "but I need the speed and stealth of an organization such as your own. Not to mention an organization that values discretion."

"But of course," she answered.

"Mono, if you would," Winters said to the ape.

Mono shuffled off into the darkness. He soon returned, carrying the unconscious body of the monster from the construction site.

"You see," said Winters, "I have nine more beasts like this one that should be coming to town very soon. Thirteen in all, to be exact. Coming from every corner of the globe."

Mono walked across the basement toward a large stone disk built into the floor. The disk concealed thirteen chambers. Mono opened the cagelike door of an empty chamber and dropped the beast down into a cell. It joined three other creatures that were recently captured; their eyes glowed in the darkness of the other chambers.

"But why? Why here? Why now?" Karai asked.

"Instinct, mostly," answered Winters. "They're animals at their core. And they recognize something familiar in the air, in the stars."

Winters faced Karai. "What can I say? I'm a lover of animals," he added mysteriously.

CHAPTER 10
DISCONTENT

At breakfast the next morning the Turtles were still confused, trying to figure out what went on the night before.

"What kind of animal was that?" asked Michelangelo.

"Is it just me," asked Donatello, "or did that creature look familiar?" He was flipping through a thick book entitled *Strange Creatures from Time and Space*.

"Yeah," said Michelangelo. "It looked like your mom."

"That would make her *your* mom, too, doofus," said Donatello, without looking up.

"We could have taken it if you slackers would have pitched in sooner," said Raphael.

"Fact remains, Raph, that we never should have been there in the first place," said Leonardo.

"Well, I suppose that we should have just let Mr. Monsterpuss continue to spread havoc throughout the city," said Raphael. "Good call, fearless leader."

Donatello looked up from his book. "And it was pretty strange to see the Foot there. And who was that woman? She was just as good a swordsman as you, Leo."

Leonardo ignored Donatello and responded to Raphael. "What, this is my fault now? Am I the only one who has to be responsible?"

"Hey, you're the *trained master*, not me," said Raphael.

"Ool-cay it-ay! Inter-splay!" Michelangelo quickly interjected, trying to avoid a physical confrontation.

The Turtles fell silent as Splinter entered the kitchen.

"Good morning, my sons," he said cheerily.

"Morning, *Sensei*," said the Turtles.

"Here you go, master," said Leonardo, "green tea, just the way you like it."

"Thank you, my son," said Splinter, smiling, as he took the cup from Leonardo. "If anyone needs me, I'll be watching my stories."

Splinter walked out of the kitchen. A moment later the TV turned on.

Raphael glared at Leonardo. *"Just the way you like it,"* he said mockingly.

"Hothead," said Leo.

"Splinter junior," Raphael retorted.

Donatello gestured with his head. "Hey, listen. The television."

The Turtles entered the living room quietly and stood behind the couch where Splinter sat.

"And in the latest in a string of strange criminal activities, a construction site was nearly destroyed last night. Authorities believe the vigilante Nightwatcher to be responsible," said a reporter, who was standing in front of the construction site.

The Turtles looked at each other without saying a word.

The news report continued. "Witnesses described the sounds coming from the structure as 'scary and animalistic.' Several individuals were seen leaving the site. However, no one could confirm the identities of the suspects. Again, anyone with any clues as to the Nightwatcher's identity are urged to contact officials as soon as possible."

Splinter turned around. "I believe you boys have some explaining to do," he said.

"Busted!" Michelangelo exclaimed.

"Kneel and explain," ordered Splinter.

The Turtles humbly told their master the details of their encounter with the Foot and the monster. Splinter was not impressed.

"Leonardo, I am most disappointed in you. You are the leader of your brothers. I was counting on you to bring order to the chaos of this family."

"But master," said Leonardo, "how can I be expected to do so when Raph—"

"There are no excuses when one is a leader," Splinter said sharply, adding, "but the involvement of the Foot and their mysterious leader worries me."

"Me, I'm worried about a monster running around the streets of New York," said Michelangelo. "But hey, that's just me."

"We have to go out and find who's responsible for this. There ain't no other solution," said Raphael.

"Raphael," said Splinter, "there are better ways to use your skills of ninjitsu. Fact gathering. Analysis. Observation. Direct contact should only be your last resort."

"Wow, that just sounds so . . . exciting," muttered Raphael.

"Save the brute vigilante junk for that Nightwing guy," said Leonardo.

"Night*watcher*," Raphael and Michelangelo said together.

"Whatever," said Leonardo.

With that comment, Raphael had had enough. "I'm goin' out," he said, leaving his brothers kneeling before Splinter.

CHAPTER 11

DARKNESS WEAVES

"Report," Winters said to General Aguila.

The Stone General stood at attention, the eaglelike shape of his upper body casting a wide shadow on the wall behind Winters.

"Lethargo the sloth has been captured," Aguila replied. "As have Lupa the werewolf and the Yeti."

"Seven down, six to go," noted Winters. He walked to his window and looked up at the night sky. "We still have time," he said softly, before asking, "And the Foot, have they been of much help to you?"

Hesitating for just a moment, Aguila said, "Yes, the Foot have been invaluable in terms of herding, blocking off exits, running interference between our hunts and the world of man. They have kept us from being seen. It goes well."

Winters stared at his General and smiled. "It's

good to see you in action again, General."

"It is good to be in action again," agreed Aguila, then bellowed with a laugh that sounded like thunder.

Across the city, Casey's stomach twisted and rumbled with anxiety. He couldn't stop thinking about April and what their troubles might mean.

"Want a little action tonight, Casey?" asked April.

"Huh? What?" mumbled Casey in surprise as he quickly put down the newspaper he had been reading and accidentally spilled a bag of potato chips onto the floor.

"You want to spar a bit tonight?" asked April.

Casey turned to face April. She was dressed in skin-tight workout gear. She pointed a bokken—a wooden training katana—at Casey.

"Oh, nah. Ever since you started with the blade weapons you, um . . . you kinda scare me," he answered.

"Suit yourself," said April. She caught sight of the newspaper's headline: "Nightwatcher Foils Arson Attempt."

Cowabunga! It's party time!

WHO IS THE NIGHTWATCHER?
Police Seek Man Known as "The Nightwatcher" for Questioning

Casey pointed his bat at the Nightwatcher. "The class is Pain 101," he said. "Meet your instructor—Casey Jones."

Raphael watched from the doorway as Splinter greeted Leonardo on his return from the jungle.

Max Winters told April about the legend of Yaotl and the Four Stone Generals.

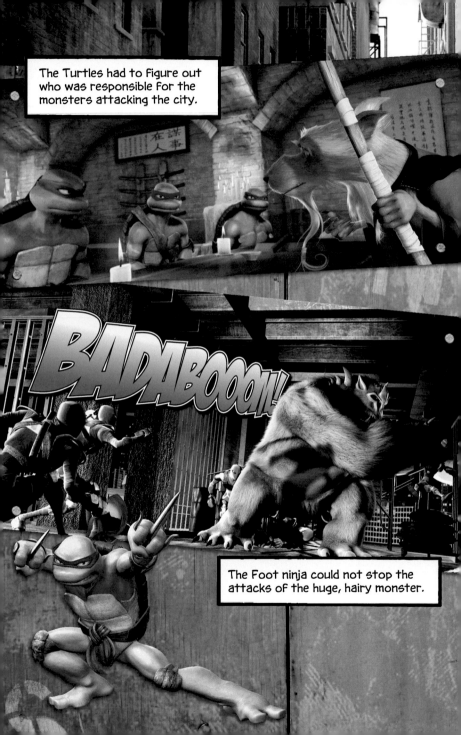

It was all in a night's work for The Nightwatcher. After fighting off a bizarre creature at Pete's Diner, he challenged Leonardo to a duel. He knew all of Leonardo's fighting techniques!

The Stone Generals agreed that Leonardo would suit their purpose.

Raphael told Master Splinter what had happened to Leonardo.

"We're going to storm the castle, rescue our brother, and save New York City . . . together," Raphael declared.

The lobby of Winters Tower, where the final battle would take place

The Turtles faced the ultimate challenge:
working together to defeat the Stone Generals.

"You miss it, don't you?" she asked. "The excitement of being a vigilante."

"Nah," he said, not sounding convincing. "No way. I mean, everyone's got to grow up some time, right?"

Casey and April looked at each other for a moment.

"Case?"

"Yeah?"

"Are you happy? I mean, with your life. With me."

Casey looked down at the potato chips, then back at April.

"Yeah. Sure," he replied, choosing the easiest possible answer, then asked, "You?"

April looked at the bokken, then at Casey.

"Yeah," she said, also trying to keep the mood light.

They stood in silence for another minute before Casey, unable to stand the awkwardness, headed for a window.

"I'm going out for some air," he said, climbing onto the fire escape. A minute later Casey was up on the roof. He looked around to make sure that he was alone, then he reached into a chimney flue and pulled out a duffel bag.

Withdrawing a baseball bat and a hockey mask, he greeted them. "Hi, boys," he said, putting on the mask. He picked up the bat and swung it a few times, and then a movement several rooftops away caught his eye. It looked like two figures were scuffling—one of them dressed in the dark motorcycle leather outfit of the Nightwatcher.

"I can't breathe!" said the Nightwatcher's victim, gasping as his leather-clad opponent slowly released his arm from around the man's throat, just enough for him to cough out an apology. "I'm sorry, man! I won't ever do it again! I'm sorr—ooof!"

But the Nightwatcher wasn't satisfied. He slammed a leather fist into the burglar's back, knocking him over an air-conditioning duct. And as the man scrambled to his feet, the Nightwatcher was ready with another attack.

"Funny how you jerks don't care about crossing the line until someone else does it . . . all over your head!" the Nightwatcher said, picking the man up by the front of his shirt. He flung the shaking, tearful man into a roof access door.

"Boy, oh boy, did you pick the wrong night to be a criminal," added the Nightwatcher.

"Hey, champ," came a voice from behind the

Nightwatcher, "don't you think you're being a little rough on the guy?"

The Nightwatcher turned away from the burglar. Under his disguise, Raphael groaned when he saw who was speaking to him.

Casey leaped forward. "You that Nightwatcher fella?" asked. "A little smaller than I expected."

Casey didn't wait for an answer. Poking the Nightwatcher in the chest with his baseball bat, he said, "I'm talkin' to you, pal. You think you own these rooftops? Well, let me teach you a thing or two."

He raised his bat. "The class is Pain 101. Meet your instructor . . . Casey Jones."

Casey swung his bat at the Nightwatcher, but the Nightwatcher was quick to spin his chain, wrapping it around the bat in one seemingly effortless move. Stalemate.

The Nightwatcher finally spoke. "You keep on playing with fire, you might just get burned," he said, before lifting his visor and looking at Casey with a mischievous grin.

Casey stared at the Nightwatcher's face and costume, jaw open in disbelief. "Raph? Is that you?" he asked. "What are you doing? Are you pretending to be . . . ?"

Casey pulled off his hockey mask and scratched his chin, feeling very confused. "But why would you?"

Then all of a sudden he connected the dots. "Oh. So that would mean . . . ," Casey said.

Raphael smiled. "Yep."

At that moment, Casey spotted the burglar trying to sneak away. "Hey," he said, looking at Raphael. Without saying anything else, they both smiled at each other. Casey pulled on his hockey mask, and Raphael lowered his visor. They sprinted toward the fleeing burglar, then quickly tackled him before coming up with an idea.

A short while later a crowd of people gathered, unsure of what to make of Raphael and Casey's handiwork. They looked and pointed up at a figure, bound by chains and dangling upside down from a street lamp.

Several blocks away, Raphael and Casey sat high up on the ledge of a building, alongside a row of stone gargoyles.

"I just got tired of sitting around waiting for some disaster to cross our paths," Raphael told Casey. "Of us battling Utroms and Triceratons or any other stupid alien . . . when there was still some guy gettin' mugged one hundred feet above the lair.

"It just didn't seem right. Especially if we had the means to do something about it. Turns out I was the only one willing to do something about it. So I saved up, bought and tweaked a sweet bike, fitted the costume, tricked out the helmet with a built-in police scanner, and began moonlighting," he said, before adding with a hint of pride, "Papers called me the 'Nightwatcher,' so I went with it."

"The guys, they ever catch on?" Casey asked.

"You kiddin' me?" scoffed Raphael. "Leo's been away for, like, forever. And the other two square shells are so wrapped up in their party business they'd never notice."

Casey nodded his head, seeming to understand what Raphael had been going through.

"What about you?" Raphael asked. "How's things with April?"

"They're good, I guess. I don't know. Seems like all I do lately is just make her upset. She used to laugh so much. Now it's mostly just working all day and coming home to tell me how much I screw up," answered Casey.

He pointed to his hockey mask. "She doesn't like me doing this. And I know she's pretending not to know that I'm out tonight. But she knows. And she knows I know she knows." Casey looked out at the city. "Life just kinda got suddenly complicated, you know?"

"You're tellin' me," agreed Raphael.

The warm, pleasant exchange of the two old friends was suddenly disrupted by a strange scream.

"What was that?" they asked.

Raphael pulled down his visor. Then, climbing onto the roof in the hope of spotting the source of the scream, they heard it once more. This time, Raphael didn't need to wait for any more proof that there was trouble. "For old time's sake?" he asked Casey.

"Ah, what the shell," replied Casey, putting on his hockey mask.

The two ran across the rooftops in the direction of the screaming, stopping when they could no longer hear it.

"I think we lost it," said Casey, slowing down.

"It's gotta be around here somewhere—," said Raphael.

Screeeeech! A large batlike creature rose up from the far side of the building, its thirty-foot wings spread out like a very large, ominous dark cloud.

"What the—?" yelled Casey, as the creature flew directly at them.

Thunka-thunka-thunka! Suddenly three large tranquilizer darts struck the back of the creature's neck.

Choom! A grappling hook wound around the creature's feet, pulling it down and back out of sight below rooftop level.

"What's going on, Raph?" asked Casey, trying his best not to freak out.

"Did I mention that me and my brothers ran into a monster last week?" said Raphael in response.

The two inched closer to the building's edge and peeked over. In the alley below, four huge figures were pummeling the giant bat with their fists and weapons. Foot Ninjas stood guard at both ends of the alley.

"The Foot!" whispered Casey. "I thought they were history! And what about those walking statues? When were you going to tell me about those?"

"Hey, those dudes are a first for me, too," said Raphael.

Down below, General Mono effortlessly picked up a Dumpster and walloped the creature with one blow, knocking it unconscious. The four Generals then picked up the bat and placed it in their transport vehicle, a hollowed-out Hummer.

Just as they were about to drive off, Casey sidled

forward for a better view, accidentally dislodging a loose piece of mortar from the roof's edge. It fell and struck a garbage can lid with a loud, hollow *clang*.

The Four Generals froze. Then they slowly looked up—right at Casey and Raphael.

"Witnesses," said General Gato.

General Aguila lifted his tranquilizer gun and fired at Casey.

Instinctively Raphael dove to shield Casey, and took a hit on his shell. "Aaargh!" he cried out in pain.

"Fetch," Aguila said to Gato. The other two Generals looked out from the Hummer and laughed.

"That can't be good," said Casey.

"No, it can't," agreed Raphael. He took out two ninja smoke pellets and threw them on the floor. *Fwoom!* Thick smoke spread out, creating a dark wall and giving them enough time to scoot inside a rooftop shack.

Suddenly Gato bounded onto the roof and strode through the smoke. He sniffed the air, then leaped straight at the shack, smashing into its steel door. *Boom!*

Inside the shack, Raphael and Casey were pressing all their weight against the door, trying to keep Gato out.

Gato pounded the door with a shoulder before raking it with his claws. The door began to collapse.

"Our beans are baked," said Casey, "the door's gonna give!"

Gato grinned, readying his final assault on the door when the beam of a police helicopter searchlight circled across the rooftop. A light on Gato's exosuit began to strobe. It was his signal to return home. Snarling at the shack, he bounded off.

After a few moments of quiet, Casey and Raphael fell out of the shack. They both looked like they had been through the worst night of their lives.

"Okay, so it was great seein' you again, Raph," Casey said. "Raph?"

Casey turned around to find Raphael passed out on the floor.

"I gotta get you someplace safe, pal," Casey said. "And then, I gotta go buy me some new undies."

CHAPTER 12
PUZZLING EVIDENCE

"**H**is vital signs seem to be okay," observed Donatello.

He lifted one of Raphael's eyelids and shone a light on it. "Pupil dilation is normal."

"Get . . . off . . . me," Raphael growled weakly, trying to push Donatello's hand away.

"Temper is normal too," Donatello said, looking up at Casey, April, Michelangelo, and Leonardo. Casey had called the Turtles after bringing Raphael to his apartment. "He's going to be fine, health wise, I mean. Otherwise, he's still the same old Raph."

Then he saw the stone disk in his brother's shell. "Whoa, what's this?"

Donatello pulled out the disk with a pair of pliers and held it up for all to see. "Some sort of stone, probably obsidian," he said. "There's an engraving on it. Looks . . . Latin American. Aztec? No. Mayan? No, definitely not. Hmm . . . but this was probably the tranquilizer dart."

April looked at the disc and swallowed hard. "It *can't* be," she said.

"What can't be, April?" asked Donatello.

"It's just a myth," she replied. "A legend. Four statues I found in the rain forests of Central America," she said.

She took the disk from Donatello. "It can't be," she repeated, sitting down on the floor.

Casey leaned down toward April. "Would it help if I said that Raph and I were chased by one of those statues you collected for that Winters guy?" asked Casey.

April's jaw dropped open.

"What are you talking about, Casey?" interjected Leonardo.

"Just some story this Winters guy told us. It all started down in Latin America. Long before the Ashmecks and the Macaroons."

"Aztecs and Mayans," corrected April.

"That's what I said," replied Casey.

April looked up at Casey. "Sit down, Jones," she said,

before recounting the legend that Max Winters had told her.

"So there was this guy named Yaotl," she began.

When she finished, Michelangelo stared at her. "Well, what next?" he asked.

"That's it. No one knows. The legend stops there," answered April, before adding, "and it's just a legend." She looked over at Casey. Sure enough, he had fallen asleep again.

Donatello studied the dart through his magnifying goggles. "The microtech of this dart is astounding," he said. "The molybdenum is of a grade found only in a few select markets, not to mention its current value is going for a little more than two grand an ounce on the futures market. At least as of this morning."

Donatello looked up from the disk—at everyone's surprised faces.

"What? I dabble in the market, is all," he said in response.

"So what we have is someone with a lot of money," noted Leonardo.

"And access to technology and the means to produce it to very exacting specs," added Donatello.

"Someone with a keen interest in these monsters

and them four stone jokers," said Raphael, now fully re-covered.

"It all points to the Winters Corporation," said Donatello.

"How do you figure that, Donnie?" asked Leonardo.

"Hello? *Genius*, remember?" Donatello said, tap-ping his temple. "Well, that and the fact that this little part of the disk has the Winters Corporation logo on it," he added with a grin.

Leonardo looked out the window. "So do you think he's trying to re-create the events from back then?" he asked.

"Well," said Raphael, "what would *you* do with an army of monsters?"

"Aside from creating my own wrestling league, I don't know," replied Michelangelo. "Maybe take over the world?"

"Guys! Not every suspicious-looking man is an alien or some sort of mutant freak trying to destroy the planet!" said April, annoyed. "It's a legend. A *legend*!"

"Do you mean *legend* in the sense of the humun-gous hair ball that attacked us?" asked Michelangelo.

"Or *legend* like in the giant bat and living statues

that attacked me and Casey?" asked Raphael.

April sighed. She didn't know what else to say. "Okay, fine. I'll help you—until we prove that you're all insane."

"Or until we prove that Winters is up to something more than merely collecting art," said Leonardo, turning away from the window.

"I'll work with April and see if those Stars of Kikin can give us any clues," Donatello said.

Raphael shook his head. "I say we just storm the castle and face this jerk in person!"

"No, Raph," Leonardo warned. "We hang back, analyze, and formulate a plan. *Then* we storm the castle. Are we clear?"

Raphael glared at his brother. "Yeah. Crystal." Feeling dissatisfied, he headed for the apartment door.

Casey stopped him. "Hey, Raph. Don't do it, man." He moved closer to the Turtle so no one else could hear. "I spent my whole life running out of rooms, ticked off at the world," Casey confessed. "I wish I could take most of it back. Sometimes taking a breather is the best thing to do, bro."

Raphael knew Casey was right but wasn't about to admit it. "Yeah, whatever," he said, as he walked out and slammed the door behind him.

Later, high up on a rooftop, Raphael looked up at the stars and took a deep breath. I have to take a breather, thought Raphael. Just have to clear my head, the only way I know how. . . .

CHAPTER 13
THE COSMIC CLOCK

Winters was standing on his roof gazing at the stars. The snakelike arcs of the Stars of Kikin were moving into closer alignment, straightening with each passing night.

Soon, he thought, very soon. He walked down the private stairwell that led to his penthouse and entered the study, passing ornately framed pictures and photographs that spanned the centuries—family, friends, and loved ones.

Settling into his favorite armchair in front of a blazing fireplace, Winters filled a snifter with cognac and lifted the glass. "To picking up the pieces," he said softly.

He took a sip, remembering the old man, now long dead, from whom he had bought the handcrafted liquor. Then he turned his gaze to the suit of armor above the fireplace, the armor of Yaotl the Conqueror.

"What is it?" Winters suddenly asked out loud.

In the darkness of the entryway stood Aguila. "Only two creatures remain, my lord," stated the General.

Winters closed his eyes. "Well, by all means then. Let's finish it. And you will finally be free of your stone prison."

"To finally fulfill our destiny," said Aguila before leaving the room.

Back in the lair, April and Donatello sat at the kitchen table poring over stacks of thick books, some of them very old. Behind them, Leonardo was pacing, lost in thought.

"So it looks like Winters is using the stars to open up a portal to another world," said April. This was the closest she had come to admitting that there was more to Winters's story than simply being a legend.

"And if we interpret these Aztec calendars correctly," continued Donatello, "we should be able to figure out where and when the next alignment will occur."

April finished the calculation. "Almost three thousand years on the nose," she said.

Michelangelo zoomed into the kitchen on his skateboard. "So it's like Haley's Comet, except that monsters come out?"

April and Donatello exchanged glances and nodded.

Leonardo finally stopped pacing. "Someone should go get Raph. It's about time he grew up and finished his little tantrum," he said angrily.

Donatello agreed. "Good idea, Leo. We should be done here soon."

Just as Leonardo was about to leave the room, Splinter walked in. He placed a hand on the Turtle's shoulder. "Leonardo, of all the virtues of leadership, empathy and understanding are among the most important," the master advised. "Your brother is in much need of this."

"Yes, *Sensei*," said Leonardo, biting back his anger as he exited the lair and entered the sewer tunnels.

CHAPTER 14
CONFRONTATIONS

The Nightwatcher stood silently on the water tower, waiting for trouble to brew. And he didn't have to wait long. A report came through on the police-band signal in his helmet.

"Attention, all on-duty officers. Report of a disturbance at Pete's Diner, Thirty-second and Tenth. No local units available. I repeat, no local units available," said the dispatcher.

The Nightwatcher jumped off the water tower and onto the rooftop below. Looking east, he could just make out the neon sign of the diner one block away. He ran as fast as he could.

Whack! The Nightwatcher kicked in the front door of the diner, poised catlike, ready for anything. The diner's sole occupant was its cook, crouched behind the counter, frantically pushing an alarm button.

Over the sound of the alarm, the Nightwatcher heard chewing and snarling sounds coming from behind the thick door of the walk-in freezer. He carefully opened the freezer door, not sure what he was going to find.

Inside the freezer a small, monkeylike creature with two horns on its head was huddled over slabs of frozen meat. The ferocious way it was tearing and chewing at the meat seemed in stark contrast to the baby-animal cuteness of its round face and big eyes. The creature did not stop chewing as it looked up at the Nightwatcher.

The Nightwatcher extended a hand. "Aww, hey there, little fella. Aren't you cute? All that commotion for just little ol' youuuuuuuu—"

The monster bit the Nightwatcher's hand, clamping its mouth down firmly—and wouldn't let go.

"Get off me! Let go!" yelled the Nightwatcher, reeling backward with the creature still attached to his hand. Plates, glasses, and utensils began to fly everywhere, smashing and breaking, as the two tumbled out of the freezer and into the diner's counter area.

The Nightwatcher struck the monster over the head with an iron skillet, and it finally let go. He took out two spiked brass knuckles from his belt and placed his fingers through them just before the creature sprang at him. The Nightwatcher managed to smack it away, into the cash register, which smashed to the floor. Coins spilled everywhere.

Seconds later the creature was back in his face, chomping and snarling. The Nightwatcher pulled out several smoke pellets and stuffed them into the creature's mouth.

Poomph! Poomph! The pellets exploded. Smoke shot out of the monster's nostrils, ears, and eyes, causing it to shriek and run out of the diner.

"Yeah! That's what I thought, you filthy little monkey!" he taunted. "No one messes with the Nightwatcher!"

The Nightwatcher turned to pick up the cash register as the cook scrambled out from a cabinet. "P-p-please don't hurt me!" he begged.

"Whaddaya talkin' about? I just *saved* you!" said the Nightwatcher as he tried to hand the cash register to the frightened cook. "Here ya go, pal. Make sure this stays safe."

But the cook was too frightened. "Take it! Just take it! Just don't hurt me, please!"

"Listen!" yelled the Nightwatcher, "I don't want your cash! I just saved your life!"

The Nightwatcher turned to place the cash register back in its spot on the counter when suddenly—*Shink!* A throwing star found its mark on the cash register, an inch from the Nightwatcher's hand.

He looked out the diner window and clearly saw Leonardo standing on the rooftop across from the street. "This just keeps getting better and better," he said before bolting through the rear door.

Leonardo somersaulted onto the street and ran after the Nightwatcher. The chase took the two down sidewalks and back alleys. Leonardo hurled an assortment of throwing stars at the Nightwatcher, and they each missed their target. But he was gaining on the mysterious vigilante.

The Nightwatcher dashed out into the busy traffic of Eleventh Avenue, jumping over passing cars and leaping from roof to roof. Leonardo crossed the avenue stealthily and just as fast, swinging from power lines and lampposts.

Finally the Nightwatcher climbed up a fire escape, all the way to the top. But he reached a dead end. The rooftop was surrounded by much taller buildings.

The Nightwatcher turned—and faced Leonardo.

"I want you to know that I appreciate your

intentions," began Leonardo, "but you can't change the world like this."

Raphael stared at his brother through his visor. The police scanner in his helmet was damaged in the fight with the monster so now Raphael heard nothing but white noise. But although he couldn't hear what Leonardo was saying, he could tell that his brother was giving him a lecture. And Raphael wanted to laugh.

". . . so I'm going to give you one chance to just walk away and stop this vigilante nonsense," Leonardo finished.

Not getting the response he wanted, Leonardo unsheathed his twin katana blades. This time Raphael reacted, pulling out twin bolos and swinging them around.

"Look," said Leonardo. "Trust me when I tell you, you don't want to do this."

Raphael charged at his brother and a bolo swung out to slap Leonardo across the face. Leonardo grabbed hold of the weapon and yanked his opponent within arm's reach. He punched the side of the Nightwatcher's helmet, cracking it, and the Nightwatcher retaliated with a swift kick.

The two circled like tigers. Every time Leonardo made an offensive move, the Nightwatcher was able to counter it. Raphael knew all of his brother's fighting techniques, and a frustrated Leonardo could not understand why he couldn't gain the upper hand.

After several minutes, Leonardo considered the situation. He decided to put into practice something he had recently learned: He would change his strategy to one of nonstrategy.

Bounding forward in a classic ninjitsu move, Leonardo stopped short of completing it. Instead he simply landed a powerful uppercut on the Nightwatcher's jaw.

The Nightwatcher's helmet flew off, revealing Raphael's face.

"R-Raph?" stammered Leonardo.

Raphael was furious—not because his identity had been revealed to Leonardo, but because he had been beaten by him. Deciding that the fight wasn't over, Raphael mule-kicked his brother, sending Leonardo sprawling backward.

"You're so smug!" Raphael spat as he paced around the fallen Turtle. "You think the world revolves around you, don't you? That we couldn't possibly survive without the mighty and powerful Leonardo to guide us through our problems, right?"

Leonardo got to his feet. "Oh, and this Nightwatcher thing qualifies as normal?" he retorted. "Dressing up like it's Halloween every night and risking the safety of our family? I mean, come on, Raphael. What were you thinking?"

"Don't push it, Leo. You can't leave home and come back expecting us to all bow down before your royal highness!"

"Hey, I was training! Training to be a better leader! For you! Why do you hate me for that?"

"Whoever said I wanted to be led? I should have gone on that training, and you know it!"

"You weren't ready!" Leonardo shouted. "You're impatient and hot tempered! And more important . . . I'm better than you."

Raphael stopped pacing and laughed. He reached behind his back and pulled out his twin sais. "Well, big brother, I'd have to disagree with you on that one," he said.

Leonardo looked at his brother. He did not want this to escalate into another fight. "Don't do this, Raph," he warned.

"Try and stop me," Raphael said, getting into a fight-ready stance.

Leonardo had no choice but to do the same.

Raphael made the first move and the fight began.

Punches, kicks, full body throws. Ninjitsu, Tae Kwon Do, street-fighting moves. Sais, katanas, shuriken. The brothers brought all the techniques and skills that they had learned over their lifetime together into this battle. It was an even match.

And then Raphael lost control. In one explosive burst of energy, Raphael knocked Leonardo to the ground and thrust his sais at Leonardo's swords. The katana blades snapped.

Raphael kneeled across his brother and placed a sai one-quarter inch from his brother's left eye, his whole body shaking with a fury that was so intense. . . .

And then he stopped, collapsing backward. He felt terribly ashamed at what he had almost done.

As he lay on the ground, Leonardo was not thinking of what Raphael had come so close to doing, but that Raphael had beaten him. He rose to his feet to face his brother, but Raphael was gone, already across several rooftops.

Leonardo looked down at his broken katana blades. All of a sudden—*phhht!* An obsidian disk embedded itself in Leonardo's arm. It was the same tranquilizer dart that hit Raphael.

Within seconds the Four Generals emerged from the surrounding darkness and approached the Turtle.

Leonardo, weakened by his fight against Raphael and swaying from the effects of the tranquilizer, crumpled to his knees and fell forward.

Gato sniffed at Leonardo. "It is neither monster nor human."

The Four Generals stared down at Leonardo as Karai approached, disturbed to see that the Turtle had been attacked in such a dishonorable way.

"He shall serve *our* purposes perfectly," said Aguila, smiling. "Let us inform our leader that the final creatures have been captured."

More than a half dozen rooftops away, Raphael stopped running. He could sense that something was wrong. Turning to look back in the direction where he had left his brother, he saw several figures standing over the fallen Turtle.

"Leo?" he called softly before sprinting back across the rooftops. But he was too late. The figures were gone from the roof—and they had taken Leonardo with them.

CHAPTER 15
RE-EMERGENCE

Splinter was practicing hatha yoga in the lair's dojo.

Even with all the chaos that surrounded his family since Leonardo's return, he was still able to create a space of tranquility in which to practice his yoga. His mind was at ease, his body in perfect poise—when Raphael suddenly burst into the dojo and collapsed.

Splinter rushed to his side. "Raphael? What is the matter?"

"I was out and did . . . something . . . something happened and I, I, aaargh!" Raphael ranted. He grabbed loose free weights and threw them across the floor.

"Raphael!" Splinter ordered sternly. "Kneel!"

At that command, Raphael regained his composure and dropped to his knees, sighing heavily. "I did something . . . I did something really stupid, master," he said.

"Go on," urged Splinter.

"I know why you chose him now. I know that there's a reason why he's the better son and I'm not," said Raphael. "And I think I made things worse tonight, a whole lot worse. I really screwed up. I know you must be so ashamed of me, father. I'm sorry."

Splinter positioned himself in front of Raphael.

"Raphael, you always bear the world's problems on your shoulders," Splinter said. "It is an admirable quality when you are a protector of others. But you must realize that while at times you may not be my favorite student, it does not mean that you are my least favorite son."

Raphael looked at his *sensei*. He had never considered things from this perspective.

"You are strong, passionate, and loyal to a fault," said Splinter. "These are the merits of a great leader, but only when tempered with compassion and humility."

"But, Master, I messed up big tonight. And I mean big."

Raphael reached around to withdraw Leonardo's broken katanas from his belt.

Splinter stared at the swords for a few moments. "Leonardo?" he asked.

"Yes," replied Raphael, ashamed.

Splinter nodded grimly. "Well then," he said, "I believe your brothers may be in need of a leader."

Raphael felt deeply humbled. "Thank you, father."

In the kitchen of the lair, April and Donatello were continuing to sift through their charts and adjust their calculations with each new piece of knowledge.

"So the first time that this portal was opened, the Stars of Kikin aligned," said Donatello. He drew a sketch on a tablet, and identical images appeared on the screen of his laptop. "And that's why it occurred in that specific Central American region."

"Now if we take into account the continuous rotation of Earth since then, as well as the gradual celestial shift that's occurred and been recorded over . . . well, over the course of that mountain of books," he said, gesturing toward the research material spread across the table, "we now know our new location."

Michelangelo entered the kitchen. "New location?" he asked.

April looked at the information that appeared on the laptop, then shook her head. She walked over to the couch to wake Casey before rejoining the Turtles.

"The new location," April announced, "is precisely at forty-point-seventy-four degrees latitude and seventy-three-point-nine degrees longitude."

"*Hello*," said Michelangelo, "in Turtle terms, please."

"New York City," said Donatello.

"Directly above Winters Tower," said April. "And the alignment is due to occur in precisely—"

"Precisely *tonight*," Donatello finished.

Just then Splinter and Raphael joined the group in the kitchen.

"Well, what're we gonna do?" asked Michelangelo.

Splinter looked at Raphael.

"I'll tell you what we're gonna do," Raphael said. "We're going to storm the castle and rescue our brother, and then we're gonna save New York City . . . together."

CHAPTER 16
CONVERGENCE

Dark storm clouds gathered in the sky directly above Winters Tower. Weather forecasters throughout the greater metropolitan region had been befuddled by its sudden appearance and strange localized intensity. Some were afraid of its rapidly gaining size.

Inside the tower change was taking place.

The lobby's Aztec calendar slowly split open, creating a one-hundred-foot hole in the middle of the floor, which looked directly into the cells in the secret basement.

Moments later the cells began to rise, fitting neatly into the lobby circle. And at the same time, Winters's elevator office hummed softly as it made its way down.

Winters stepped out of his office wearing the armor of Yaotl the Conqueror. In his left hand was Yaotl's helmet.

Pointing his right hand at the ceiling, Winters pressed a button on a remote control, disengaging a series of locking mechanisms.

The sound of heavy grinding and sliding accompanied the opening of a hole in the ceiling, followed by similar holes opening on every floor above it. Finally a hole opened in the roof, revealing the sky and raging storm. Winters had never felt more content than he did at this moment.

Looking at the cells, he was gratified to see that each one contained an occupant. Had he looked closer, though, he would have noticed that one cell did not contain the monster he was looking for. Instead, it held the unconscious form of Leonardo.

Across the city April and Casey finished gearing up. While Casey had put on a variety of sporting gear— football and hockey pads, protective baseball cup, bicycle touring wear—April wore sleek-fitting Japanese combat gear adorned with martial arts weapons.

"Yo, babe, have you seen my hockey mask?" asked Casey. "I could have sworn I left it here on this bookcase."

April walked up to Casey with her hands behind her back. "Why do you want that old thing," she replied, "when you could be wearing this?"

She held up a brand-new hockey mask, partially painted in warrior stripes.

"No way," said Casey, impressed.

"I was saving it for our anniversary," April said, smiling.

The two walked toward each other, the tension that had developed between them since April's return quickly evaporating

Just then a car honked. "That's our ride," said April.

"Wouldn't you know it," muttered Casey, grabbing his bag of weapons.

They exited their building, shocked to find themselves almost blown off their feet by the force of the wind.

Weather scientists were calling the storm the fiercest of the new millennium as it intensified, circling clockwise like a hurricane. An eye was beginning to open up at its center.

Inside the tower lobby Winters gazed skyward. The eye of the storm had fully blossomed, exposing the Stars of Kikin.

Winters smiled as the last star moved into alignment above the others. A bolt of light energy shot down the length of the newly formed constellation, heading for Earth—and for Winters Tower.

The beam of light entered the building and traveled down its entire length, striking the center of the thirteen monster cells. Bathed in the celestial energy, the chambers began moving about like a sliding puzzle, seeking their own proper alignment.

Moments later they started to sink into the floor. Soon Yaotl's Shadow Gate portal would open once again after three thousand years. Winters approached the outer rim of the circle and acknowledged each cell's inhabitant, thanking each monster for its return. "Finally," he said. "*Finally*!"

He strode contentedly to the thirteenth cell and suddenly stopped as he lay his eyes on not a monster, but a humanoid Turtle.

Realizing that he had been tricked by his own Generals, Winters cried out in anguish, "What have you done?"

CHAPTER 17
THE BATTLE FOR FOREVER

Karai looked up at the sky and shivered. It grows ever blacker, she thought, much like this night's dark deeds. Continuing her walk through the gardens that surrounded the base of Winters Tower, she made sure the garden's front gate was locked, then motioned a dozen Foot Ninja into various positions along the grounds.

"As ordered," she said, "no one gets in. No one interferes. No one bears witness."

At that moment a sudden pounding at the gate sent Karai motioning several Foot into taking their positions on either side of the gate. She opened the doors and looked out at Splinter, Raphael, Donatello, Michelangelo, April, and Casey.

"You've got to be kidding me," she muttered.

Within moments Karai and her nearly one hundred

Foot Ninja were in full battle against the six visitors.

The odds were to Raphael's liking. Better yet, he thought, it's completely chaotic, the way battles should be. The way battles were meant to be won.

"I am so going to enjoy this," he said as he twirled a sai in each hand and bounded forward to face two Foot Ninjas. Somersaulting over them, the Turtle twisted in midair before bringing the hilt end of his weapons down on their heads. The ninjas instantly fell to the ground.

Splinter, using his walking stick like a bo staff, thrust and parried against a Foot's katana blade. Then, with a speed more common to an animal than to a man, he spun around and used his tail to strike his opponent across the face. The ninja was stunned. Splinter attacked him once more with his walking stick, and this time the man did not get up.

Michelangelo was enjoying the challenge of the fight. He did flips off the backs of the Foot, pretended to be exhausted to draw the ninjas toward him, then launched an all-out attack on his opponents.

Donatello fought using geometry, envisioning angles of attack, creating mental diagrams of how a fight would unfold. Imagining his bo staff to be one side of a triangle and his legs as the other two sides,

Donatello altered the shape of the triangle as the battle flowed.

Casey, on the other hand, fought on pure adrenaline rush. His fight method was simple: choose a weapon and beat on the bad guy. His arsenal of weapons, which he stashed in a golf bag strapped across his back, included a hockey stick, a lacrosse stick, and two kinds of baseball bats, wooden and aluminum. Just then he was wielding his wooden bat, picturing himself hitting homers at the Foot.

It was a tactic that often worked—until now. Three Foot Ninja had him cornered against a fence. In a striking display of teamwork, one ninja swung his katana at Casey's head, causing him to duck out of his way, while another ninja used his katana to slice the baseball bat in two. Then the third ninja landed a kick across Casey's jaw, knocking him to the ground.

The ninjas raised their katanas and were about to finish him off when April appeared, cartwheeling between Casey and the Foot. Drawing her katana across the stomachs of all three ninjas, April succeeded in frightening them enough so that they backed off.

April helped Casey to his feet and handed him his aluminum baseball bat.

"I'd stick to metal bats from now on, Jones," she said.

"Thanks, babe," said Casey.

"Look!" said April, pointing. "The front door to the tower is open!"

"Guys!" Casey yelled to the Turtles and Splinter. "Let's roll!"

They ran into the lobby and Karai quickly ordered her troops to give chase.

"What do we do, dudes?" asked Michelangelo.

Casey looked around. Eyeing a priceless vase, he pulled out his hockey stick and swung at the vase, smashing it to bits. Suddenly sirens blared and security shutters came slamming down, just as they had done when he accidentally broke the other vase on his first visit. Now Karai and her ninjas were locked out.

"Nice work, Jones," April said, smiling.

Casey blushed. "I have my moments."

"Check it out!" said Donatello, pointing to the other end of the vast lobby, where strange light beams were swirling. "That would be the vortex to another world, I assume. Cool."

"Hopefully that's where we'll find Leonardo," Michelangelo said.

The group ran toward the lights and the glowing chambers, which had risen once again. Above the cells the portal grew. It was Yaotl's Shadow Gate.

Michelangelo approached a cell. "Leo? Is that you?" he called out.

A furry, clawed hand swiped at Michelangelo, forcing the Turtle to back away. "I guess that would be a no," he said.

Michelangelo quickly scanned the other cells until he found his brother. "Leo! I got him!" he called out. "One little problem, though, the cell's got a lock on it."

"Not a problem," said Donatello. "Out of the way, please."

Donatello placed a small explosive into the keyhole. Within moments the lock fell open with a sharp snapping sound.

Raphael rushed to pull Leonardo out of the cell. "Hey, buddy! Come on, man! Leo, please wake up! It's me, Raphael!"

But there was no response as Raphael held Leonardo, fearing that he was too late.

Suddenly Leonardo coughed and opened his eyes. Seeing Raphael, he asked, "What took you so long?" before slowly getting up.

Casey reached for one of Leonardo's spare katana blades in his golf bag and handed it to Raphael.

"Listen, I . . . I'm sorry," Raphael said as he handed the katana to Leonardo.

"I know," said Leonardo. "I forgive you."

The two brothers moved awkwardly to hug each other when they heard a *smash!* high above their heads. Then a figure clad in armor hurtled down toward them.

Whump! The figure slammed into the floor. It was Winters, dressed in the armor of Yaotl. Aguila stared down at the group from Winters's penthouse and snarled.

"Whoa," said Casey. "Is this guy dead or what?"

Michelangelo took Casey's hockey stick and poked at Winters' limp body.

"Yup," he answered. "He's *way* dead, dude."

At that moment Winters took a big gasp of air and sat up. Everyone jumped back. No normal being could have survived such a fall! Yet Winters had not only survived, he barely had even a scratch or a bruise on him.

"We were so close," he said in despair, "so very close."

He fell back onto the floor, with his hands covering his face. "This was our chance. We could have changed it all."

"It all ends now, Max," said April.

Winters looked up at April, registering her

presence for the first time. Glancing around he was surprised to see the group that had gathered in his lobby.

"Miss O'Neil? What's the meaning of this?" he asked.

"We know everything, Max," said April. "We know that you're trying to re-create what Yaotl started three thousand years ago."

Winters looked at April. A slight shudder rippled through his body. He removed his helmet. "There are things, Miss O'Neil, that no one could possibly know. For it was *I* who stood on that battlefield three thousand years ago. It was *I* who opened the Shadow Gate portal to that other darker world. . . . *I* who brought monsters to Earth and utter ruin to magnificent Xalica.

"*I* am Yaotl, Miss O'Neil," said Winters.

Everyone stared at him, speechless at this confession.

"And I, along with my four Generals, were made to pay a price," he continued. "Siba-Noor, Xalica's most powerful sorceress, who had been away at the time of our attack, returned as her city fell to ruin. It didn't take her long to figure out that we brought about its decimation.

"She cursed the five of us that day. My four comrades-in-arms were turned into stone. Living stone. My curse was to live . . . forever, to feel the pain of losing the ones I loved time and time again. The pain of eternity.

"We were doomed to live this way until, as Siba-Noor put it, 'You correct the mistakes of your past.'"

Winters gestured to the lobby, to the containment cells, to the sky above them.

"That's what this is about," he added. "Penance, atonement, finally getting a chance to right our wrongs."

The Four Generals stomped heavily into the room. "Our master fails to include crucial points in his tale," said Aguila. "He fails to discuss the petrified agony of three thousand years."

"Of watching the erosion of your own body throughout the centuries," growled Gato.

Winters looked at the Generals. "My brothers, I—"

"We are no brothers to you!" snapped Aguila. "Our brotherhood was broken the day that you condemned us to this eternity."

Crash! The Foot Ninja had finally broken through the lobby door. Now Karai entered cautiously and looked around, acknowledging that it was best not to say anything at this point.

Gato continued the tirade against their master. "And now, he has tired of feeding on the nectar of life, of loving his entire life, of feeling."

He gestured toward the light beams in the still-incomplete portal. "So he prefers to end it all. To end his misery at the expense of ours."

Aguila walked toward the containment cells. The portal lights grew in intensity as he added, "But thanks to his cunning, his technology, we are now capable of living. We have now become . . . *gods*."

"With one monster still free, Siba-Noor's curse will never be broken!" Gato noted.

"And we shall finish what we began all those years ago," Serpiente said. "We will finally have our victory."

Mono grunted in agreement as Aguila turned toward Winters. "Join us, Yaotl," Aguila said. "Join us and live a life eternal with us at your side and the world at your feet!"

"Never," replied Winters, unmoved by their words. "Don't you see? This was our opportunity to set things right! We were wrong those many years ago, wrong! Don't you understand?"

"No," said Aguila. "*You* were wrong. And now you are weak."

Aguila turned to Karai. "Destroy them," he ordered.

The leader of the Foot Clan considered this order. Why should she help the Stone Generals when they have only been hostile toward her and her ninjas? Karai suddenly made a series of hand gestures to the Foot Clan.

"Okay," said April, "what does *that* mean?"

"It means we're going to help *you*," answered Karai. Following her order, forty Foot Ninja ran silently out of the building, leaving four behind with Karai.

"My soldiers will find the final monster," said Karai. "But *you* will have to bring it back here. Hurry, we don't have much time."

Karai left to catch up with her ninja. April looked over at Winters. It took a single nod from him to send her sprinting off after Karai.

Casey turned to the four Foot. "I got shotgun!" he yelled, running out of the room, the four Foot falling into formation behind him.

The Generals began to move in on Winters. Seeing this, the Turtles leaped in to form a wall between them and Winters.

Aguila stepped toward Leonardo. Raphael countered by taking his place next to Leonardo and was soon joined by Michelangelo and Donatello.

"You mess with one of us," said Raphael, "you mess with all of us."

"Challenge accepted," Aguila said with a grin.

Behind them the portal lights flickered and grew brighter.

"What's with the funky effects?" asked Michelangelo.

"My guess is that the Stars of Kikin haven't reached their true alignment yet," answered Donatello.

"Meaning?"

"Meaning the portal is still forming. Probably won't be fully open for another ten minutes or so," Donatello told his brother.

"So we have ten minutes, maybe less," said Leonardo. "Let's make them count."

"I love it when you talk like that," Raphael said.

Leonardo thrust a katana at Aguila, while Raphael leaped at Mono. Gato lashed out at Michelangelo, and Serpiente lunged toward Donatello.

Winters rose to help the Turtles.

"Wait," said Splinter, as a lesion-covered tentacle momentarily shot out of the still-forming portal, narrowly missing Winters's head.

"My students must face the Generals alone," said Splinter. "As *brothers*."

Another tentacle, this one red and glowing, whipped out of the portal, again just missing Winters. It recoiled back just as quickly as it had appeared.

"You're right," said Winters, pointing at the portal. "Plus, we have more important things to do."

A small, eyeless monster had jumped out of the portal and was sniffing the air, seeking a victim. It had four arms and a single horn growing from its forehead.

Winters ran and flipped in the air, landing feet first against the creature's back, knocking it to the floor. But the monster was fast and its sense of smell was uncanny. It lashed out at Winters with its two left arms, striking the man hard across his face. But Winters quickly recovered, ducking to avoid the creature's next attack.

Using both hands, he grabbed the creature by its horn and lifted it off the ground. The monster hissed and spat. Winters swung it around in the air several times, then flung it back into the portal.

Winters smiled. It had been many years since he had last engaged in physical battle. It felt good. He stood in front of the portal, ready for the arrival of the next monster.

Splinter joined Winters, adopting a defensive

posture: feet planted firmly on the ground, arms held poised at waist level, elbows down, fists up.

About forty feet away, Donatello landed a flying dropkick against Serpiente's right shoulder and followed through with rapid-fire bo staff strikes against the Stone General's jaw. Serpiente countered with a straight jab at the Turtle's plastron, striking him hard. Donatello rolled with the blow, allowing his body to fall backward. As he fell, he spun into a cartwheel before standing once again facing Serpiente. The two began to slowly circle around each other, waiting for the chance to attack.

Off to one side of the lobby, Michelangelo leaped out of the way of General Mono's hammer. The hammer struck the floor hard, cracking it. Shards and chunks of brown marble flew in all directions.

"That'll come out of your paycheck, monkey-boy," quipped Michelangelo, before the towering, apelike Stone General swung its hammer again, this time aiming directly for the Turtle. Michelangelo stepped out of the way and then quickly rushed toward Mono, spinning both nunchakus at the General's chest and face, landing a dozen hard blows.

Mono let out a scream of outrage.

Gato's fast, thought Leonardo, too fast. The Turtle

faced Gato, looking for an opening. Then the jaguar-like Stone General blinked, and Leonardo made his move, slashing with his katana in a back-handed arc. The blade glanced off Gato's forehead, surprising him.

In a blur, Gato punched Leonardo with such force that it knocked the katana from the Turtle's hand. Leonardo landed hard into a large display case, sending pieces of wood and glass flying everywhere. Looking around for his katana, the Turtle was pleased to find a number of swords and weapons, the contents of the display case.

"Excellent selection," Leonardo said, reaching for a pair of swords twice the length of his katanas.

Raphael and Aguila parried and thrust at each other as they moved around the containment cells. They were careful not to get too close to the cells, which the imprisoned monsters were straining to escape.

As Raphael backed away from Aguila's round-house punch, he felt fur touch the back of his neck. He ducked down just as a powerfully muscled arm covered in thick white fur snatched at the air above his head.

Missing Raphael, the Yeti then reached for Aguila,

who managed to avoid the monster but fell to the floor when Raphael spun both legs out to trip him.

Raphael jumped on Aguila, attacking the Stone General with his sais. Aguila snarled as two tiny pinpricks of red light glowed from his chest. He rushed at the Turtle, but Raphael spun out of the way, and Aguila landed against a containment cell.

Furry red hands with razor-sharp talons scratched at the Stone General's shoulders. Aguila bolted from the creature's reach—right into Raphael's fists.

CHAPTER 18

THE RETURN TO FOREVER

Above Winters Tower the storm raged with the concentrated fury of a category five hurricane. Splinter and Winters stared up at the storm through the multileveled hole above their heads. The Stars of Kikin sparkled and glowed as the portal surged with renewed energy.

Just then Splinter spotted movement in one of the chambers. He quickly stepped aside as the cell slid toward the portal and locked eyes with the creature trapped within. He could see the intense fear of the giant slothlike creature. A moment later the cell shot away, sucked into the portal's vortex. Splinter shuddered at the thought of where it had gone.

"Watch out!" cautioned Winters as another containment cell flew into the portal. The high-pitched screech of a bat receded into the distance and was immediately replaced with a metallic twittering sound as a monster emerged from the portal and into the lobby.

"Dibs," said Splinter, using one of Michelangelo's favorite words. He pulled his walking stick from his belt, stepped silently up behind the creature, and tapped it on the shoulder. The monster spun around, revealing a face covered in a half dozen different color eyes. Its mouth was a gashlike scowl from which protruded two long lower canine teeth.

Splinter hit the monster with his walking stick, then pummeled it with a series of rapid karate strikes to the face. The creature jumped back in pain, closing all of its eyes, and Splinter quickly pushed it back into the portal, where it disappeared.

No sooner had the creature left than a thick cerulean tendril, the tip ending in a gnashing mouth, slithered out of the portal toward Splinter. Winters rushed over and gently moved the rat out of the way. He then picked up an Aztec war hatchet and began hacking at the tendril. The tendril whipped around wildly and withdrew into the portal, its mouth uttering curses in an alien tongue.

Three more containment cells dislodged from the lobby floor and flew into the portal. Then another, and another.

"We're running out of time," said Winters. "The portal's beginning to close!"

Hearing this, Leonardo and Raphael exchanged glances across the lobby and began moving their fights toward each other. Within minutes the two brothers stood back-to-back.

"They had better hurry with capturing that last monster," said Leonardo.

"I'm sure my man Casey's got it all under control," said Raphael.

"That's exactly what I'm afraid of!" said Leonardo.

Across the city the Cowabunga Carl party van roared around a corner, barely holding the road.

"This has got to be the worst vehicle to save the world with," said Casey, turning the steering wheel sharply. He shot a glance in the rearview mirror at the monster bounding behind them.

They had found the thirteenth monster, a huge alligator-like creature whose jaws were filled with several rows of sharp, oversize teeth. And they were now its bait!

Crammed into the back of the van along with four Foot Ninja, Karai looked at April with concern. April called out to Casey, "Better put the pedal to the metal! The monster is gaining on us!"

Back in the lobby of Winters Tower, Donatello and Michelangelo were now standing with Leonardo and Raphael.

"Gee, Raph, a few minutes ago I thought *we* were herding Gato and Aguila together," said Leonardo. "Now I think *they* were herding *us*."

Raphael scowled. It was clear that Serpiente and Mono had steered Donatello and Michelangelo toward them—and the four Turtles were surrounded.

"Listen," said Raphael. "I'm the last guy to sound like a TV cartoon, but I think we need to work *together*."

"Why Raph, no solo act tonight?" teased Leonardo.

Raphael grinned.

Splinter looked over from his position alongside the portal. His sons were a team at last.

"We're running out of time," Winters repeated, pointing at the portal. The vortex within the portal was growing weaker, and the portal was shrinking.

"An interesting choice of words for an *immortal*, Mr. Winters," said the rat.

"Winters. Maximilian Winters. What I hope is the last in a long line of false identities, of empty lives," he said, wearily. "Please, call me by my real name. Call me Yaotl."

"Yaotl," said Splinter, "all the containment cells have been sucked into the vortex."

"Yes," agreed Yaotl. No one had addressed him with that name in three thousand years.

A giant tendril suddenly lashed out at Yaotl. Giving it a powerful kick, he sent the tendril back into the portal with a howl. Then he pointed upward, frowning. "The portal grows weaker, as does the storm," Yaotl said. "The Stars of Kikin will soon pass out of alignment, and then the portal will close. And then . . . and then it will be too late. Too late to atone. . . ."

The four Ninja Turtles faced the four Stone Generals.

"Time to bring this party to a close," said Raphael.

Leonardo agreed. He raised the two long swords that had been housed in the display case. "Let's do it then."

"I love it when you dudes talk like that," smiled Michelangelo.

"Ditto, ad infinitum," nodded Donatello.

All at once, the Turtles launched their attack on

the Generals. Weapons and ninjitsu skills were pitted against stone and brute strength. Weapons parried and slashed, thrust and twirled. Standing crane positions erupted into flying dropkicks, and offensive moves were executed with grace and precision.

The Generals, indomitable in one-on-one combat, were much less successful fighting as a team. They got in one another's way and had no strategies to work off one another's strengths and weaknesses.

The Turtles, on the other hand, were unstoppable as a team. They knew how to play off one another, when to drop back and let someone else take a lead, and when to make their own signature moves.

The Generals began to make mistakes, which the Turtles turned to their advantage. Within minutes the Generals found themselves trapped in a circle, then driven back . . . toward the portal.

The portal, even in its diminished state, contained great power. It tugged at the four Generals. The howls and shrieks of the horrible monsters trying to cross over to Earth from within grew louder and more desperate.

The Generals now stood at the edge of the portal, teetering against its pull. Even the Turtles could feel the portal's force.

The Turtles nodded to one another. And in perfect sync they leaped feet first at the Generals, knocking them back into the portal. For the briefest moment the Generals seemed to hang in midair above the portal, refusing to surrender to its whirlwind embrace almost by sheer force of will.

But only for a moment. Monstrous alien tendrils darted from the vortex, plucking each General out of the air. And the Generals were gone.

The Turtles collapsed onto the lobby floor, unable to believe that the battle was finally over.

And it wasn't.

Thoom! The hands of the four Stone Generals slammed onto the ridge of the portal. The Turtles jumped back. The Generals began to pull themselves out of the portal and into the lobby.

Aguila raised his head over the edge. "Silly children," he said, pulling himself up. "We are immortals made of stone! The Earth has only *begun* to feel our wrath!"

The Turtles stood at the ready, weapons in hand. They were now joined by Splinter and Yaotl.

"This ends here," said Yaotl. "This ends *now*."

Ignoring his words, the four Generals lumbered forward.

Suddenly *KER-SMASH!* The outer lobby doors exploded off their hinges as the Cowabunga Carl van careened in, with the alligator-like monster just inches from its rear bumper.

"Look out!" yelled Yaotl, pushing Splinter to safety, the Turtles leaping after them.

Casey cut the wheel of the van at the last possible second before it could ram into the Generals. The van skidded sideways and smashed into a wall, coming to a sudden stop. But the alligator monster's momentum kept it moving forward. It slid across the smooth marble floor and slammed hard into the four Generals, knocking them back into the portal, and then the creature itself sailed right in behind them.

"Look," said Splinter, pointing upward.

In the sky above, the Stars of Kikin could be seen moving out of alignment. The storm clouds began to dissipate.

"It ends," said Yaotl, his gaze returning to the now-closing portal.

"No," came a voice. A *human* voice. It was Aguila.

Aguila struggled to pull himself out of what remained of the portal. Mono, Gato, and Serpiente also appeared. They looked just as they did before entering the portal—except they were no longer made of stone. They were human. The curse of immortality had been lifted, but they were eternally doomed to pain and suffering if they remained in the portal.

"You cannot defeat us!" Aguila cried out.

Wham! Without a moment's hesitation, Leonardo and Raphael launched a series of roundhouse kicks and pushed the Generals back into the portal. Then a blinding shaft of light erupted and the Generals' screams could be heard as the portal exploded, spinning funnel-like upward and then disappearing.

"We did it," said Raphael. "We did it!"

The four Turtles high-fived each other as Splinter smiled proudly.

The doors of the van *clanged* to the ground, and its passengers piled out. Casey appeared first, falling to the ground groggily. Then Karai spilled out on top of Casey, followed by April, who pushed Karai aside.

Casey hugged April and they kissed for a long time.

"Aww," said Michelangelo, happy that the two had finally made up.

Raphael and Leonardo hugged each other, their own battle now behind them.

Karai stepped forward and bowed briefly. "You

are every bit the warriors I was informed you were," she said. "You have passed."

"Passed what?" asked Leonardo.

"You know us?" asked Raphael.

"I've known of you for some time," she answered.

Karai walked away and rejoined her Foot Ninja. "Savor your victory tonight. For soon we will have further business together. The kind that involves familiar faces from your past."

Smiling mysteriously, she threw something to the ground. Thick smoke rose instantly and filled the room. When it cleared, Karai and the Foot were gone.

April looked around and saw her former boss hunched over in a corner. He was sobbing.

"Max, what's wrong?" she asked.

Yaotl's sobbing turned to laughter as he held up a hand smeared with blood—his own blood.

"I'm never usually *that* happy to be bleeding," said Michelangelo.

"You would be if you were an immortal who couldn't bleed for three thousand years," Donatello said.

Yaotl stood up and faced the group. "Thank you,"

he said. "Thank you from the bottom of my heart. You've made a very old man very, very happy."

Then sitting down, he smiled as wind blew in, bringing with it the scent of flowers from the garden. "Peace at last," murmured Yaotl as his flesh and bone began to age and turn to dust, thousands of years slipping away in the space of a heartbeat.

The wind carried away Yaotl's dust. And all that remained of the mighty conqueror was an empty suit of armor.

EPILOGUE

Raphael knocked on the open door to Splinter's room. "You wanted to see me, *Sensei*?" he asked.

Splinter was kneeling on the floor of the candlelit room. Incense filled the air. "Sit down, Raphael," Splinter said.

Raphael knelt and bowed his head. "Thank you, Master Splinter, for your guidance," he said softly. "I can only hope that one day I will be able to begin the next stage of my training like Leo."

Splinter smiled. He reached into the open box next to him and withdrew a medallion. It was similar to the one he had given to Leonardo when he returned from the rain forest.

"That, my son," said Splinter, "you have already accomplished. Our training works in mysterious ways. There are many questions along the way. But the answer that lies in all of our questions . . . is *family*."

Raphael was overjoyed. Accepting the medallion from his master, the Turtle stood up and quietly left the room, feeling more excitement than he had in a very long time.

Splinter looked past Raphael into the darkness of the hallway outside his room. And his eyes met Leonardo's.

The two exchanged knowing smiles, pleased with the way things turned out.

"So what makes a family? Personally, it's more than sharing a roof or a bathroom. It's sharing life. *Life.* My father taught me that, and I think it's pretty much true. Pretty much, providing you don't kill each other in the process. Hey, nobody said it was easy, right?"

—*Raphael the Turtle*